MASTER STRATEGIST

Alan Clifton is a management professional with more than two decades of international experience in the corporate sector. He has worked across diverse industries such as automotive, Information Technology, education, publishing and healthcare. He has also been part of critical projects with the Government of India, international non-profits and the private sector. Alan is interested in marketing, strategy and communications. He is a graduate in Physics and has a Masters in Mass Communication. He has also earned a PhD in Science and Technology Studies from one of South Asia's most reputed schools of Economics in Delhi, India.

MASTER STRATEGIST

Leadership To Drive Change and Innovation

ALAN CLIFTON

Published by
Rupa Publications India Pvt. Ltd 2019
7/16, Ansari Road, Daryaganj
New Delhi 110002

Sales centres:
Allahabad Bengaluru Chennai
Hyderabad Jaipur Kathmandu
Kolkata Mumbai

Copyright © Alan Clifton 2019

The views and opinions expressed in this book are the author's own and the facts are as reported by him which have been verified to the extent possible, and the publishers are not in any way liable for the same.
All rights reserved.

No part of this publication may be reproduced, transmitted, or stored in a retrieval system, in any form or by any means, electronic, mechanical, photocopying, recording or otherwise, without the prior permission of the publisher.

ISBN: 978-93-5333-569-4

First impression 2019

10 9 8 7 6 5 4 3 2 1

The moral right of the author has been asserted.

Printed at HT Media Ltd, Gr. Noida

This book is sold subject to the condition that it shall not, by way of trade or otherwise, be lent, resold, hired out, or otherwise circulated, without the publisher's prior consent, in any form of binding or cover other than that in which it is published.

*Dedicated to my dad, Amalendu K.C.,
a military hero, an outstanding strategist
and my greatest influence.*

CONTENTS

Prologue ix

1. The Anatomy of Strategy 1
2. Master Strategists—The Transformers 12
3. Mastering Strategic Thinking 36
4. Deploying Strategies in Corporate Organizations 60
5. Design Thinking and Strategic Design Thinking 75
6. Using Game Theory to Formulate Strategies 86
7. Modern Theories of Organizational Strategy 95
8. Conclusion 112

Bibliography 117

PROLOGUE

In 2001, Stevens, a successful businessman and investor from California, began exploring avenues across the world to expand his business investments. One of his friends advised him to explore investment opportunities in India, as the country, he was told, holds great potential for investors looking for high returns and stable growth.

Convinced, Stevens landed in Mumbai, India's finance capital. For over a month he attended meetings, participated in VC clubs and tried to network with grass-roots entrepreneurs. It was on one such occasion that he was advised to visit the Barak Valley, a far-flung region in South Assam that boasted of lush tea gardens and several new agro-forestry initiatives. Armed with these details, Stevens landed in Silchar one sunny day. There, he spent about two weeks travelling across the valley and meeting all kinds of people. After considerable review, Stevens was sure that he wanted to invest in one of the defunct tea gardens founded by a British company in the late 1880s.

However, in just over a year, Stevens realized that his investment decision had been wrong, as much as his inability to assess the people who had been advising him all the while. Despite varied advice and his own experiences in investment, he was unable to succeed. There was something very significant that he had overlooked in the whole episode.

Although scholars from across the world have dabbled in

strategy for a long time, the subject remains elusive. The insights we have gathered on the subject so far are situation-specific and therefore grossly inadequate to meet the expansionist needs of most businesses and individuals.

There is no holy grail that can provide us a structured understanding of how superior strategy is framed and deployed. It possesses characteristics of both science and the arts and requires a superior application of the mind. Good strategy emerges from a complex maze of thoughts, experiences and interjections.

Strategy is crucial to all human endeavours—from managing individual careers to managing communities, or from spearheading organizations to managing nations or international affairs. In all these situations, strategy serves as a guiding light and enables us to navigate unique situations in order to realize a specific set of goals. Without the insights of strategy, the goals would remain an impossible, distant dream. The idea for this book cropped up during my experiences in the corporate world, an environment of cut-throat competition. My role as a corporate leader in Marketing and Communications helped me appreciate the significance of visionary leadership. Over the years I realized that every organizational success is a direct outcome of the key strategist who drove its vision.

My earliest memory of a master strategist is that of my father, a veteran officer who served in a unique military organization that had a dual role—of securing the nation from external aggression as well as maintaining internal peace. As a responsible officer he deployed countless operational strategies in the face of challenges. There were soldiers and officers who were exhausted from prolonged military operations and had to be kept motivated. Then there were the demands of the aspirational political class, who tried to interfere in military affairs, as well as a rapidly changing geopolitical milieu. In managing such complex situations, I saw my dad develop strategies that could serve as win-win propositions. These strategies were usually multi-layered and emergent, i.e., they changed with changing contexts. As a strategist, he possessed unique traits. He was sensitive, meticulous, focused and ruthless—all of which were required to prepare the essential concoction that makes strategists stand out. One of the greatest lessons dad left behind for me was the need to nurture a strong survivor spirit and an infectious zeal for executing tasks with perfection.

The book is also inspired by countless other acquaintances, friends and strangers I have met across the world—in Silicon Valley of California, in Tokyo, or in the emerging business hubs of Berlin. Wherever I travelled, I was humbled by amazing types of strategic leadership that were poised to bring about such a wide array of societal and organizational change.

This book intends to kindle the strategic thinker in you. The chapters in the book are structured so as to enable you to gather an almost 360 degree view of strategy. The book is simultaneously prescriptive and informative, and its underlying intent is to help you start your journey towards becoming a master strategist who can drive extraordinary results.

The book would remain incomplete if I do not mention the contribution of my family members. I am grateful to my mother, my wife and my daughter for their unstinted support and encouragement. I would also like to thank the brilliant editorial team members at Rupa Publications, India, for their commendable efforts in producing such a good read.

Alan Clifton

1
THE ANATOMY OF STRATEGY

Over a period of 150,000 years, the one characteristic that has nurtured human existence is the ability of human beings to withstand challenges. This ability to survive and thrive is largely attributed to the enhancement of human cognition and its application in everyday lives. It was during this evolutionary phase that strategy slowly emerged, to become the driver of human civilization.

Imagine a game of football where the primary objective is to navigate through hurdles and structures to score goals. Every player in the match has to operate tactically and contribute to the collective by positioning themselves in places from where they can steer the football to their team's advantage. The players who are able to align themselves to the needs of the collective thrive, while the ones who fail to do so pull down the performance of their team. In this, the football match can be seen as a battle of strategy. The one whose strategy is superior and effective is likely to win.

Authors have offered varied definitions for strategy, although the modern use of the term is most often framed around organizations. For Igor Ansoff, a prominent Russian American mathematician and scientist, strategy is 'a set of decision rules for the company to enjoy profitable growth.' For Harvard Professor

Micheal Porter, 'The essence of strategy is choosing what not to do.' In that one line Porter nailed what is expected of strategists. Porter uses strategy in a more generic sense and 'considers it to be associated with the positioning of the company in the environment it is part of, with the aim of achieving a favourable position.' In this sense, strategy is about choice—and choosing to stick to a particular line of thinking.[1]

This particular inclination of strategy towards organizations was not always so. In the ancient world, strategy was largely associated with military warfare, as war and kingdoms were the dominant structures of the time.

Strategy in Ancient Times

In ancient Rome, the formations of the legions followed a strategic roadmap that was founded on the idea that when troops are kept together, they would be able to fight more effectively. The military commanders also realized that getting the troops to rush the enemy was not a good idea, as the success of this scheme usually depended on higher manpower or luck. It was this realization that compelled them to think of deploying strategy.

The Roman legions that were deployed came to utilize robust strategies. During battle, the legions had the cavalry, the flanks, the cohorts and the reserves arranged in a manner that offered a strategic advantage to the army. The battle formations (First Formation, Second Formation etc.) that were used for attacking varied and depended on the strengths and weaknesses of their

---

[1]Porter Michael E., How Competitive Forces Shape Strategy, published March 1979, *Harvard Business Review* https://hbr.org/1979/03/how-competitive-forces-shape-strategy Accessed May 2, 2019

own army and that of the enemy. During transit, the legions followed a different arrangement even as they kept the army in complete readiness against sudden attacks.[2]

Rome was not the only city that applied strategy in its military. In Greece, the citizens of Sparta, a city known for its valour and fighting spirit, used strategy in their everyday lives. Sparta, the capital of the Laconia region located on the Peloponnesus peninsula in modern Greece, was founded in the ninth century BCE and soon emerged as a society focused on valour. Patriotism, for the Spartans, was a means to contribute to their motherland. It was this zeal that gave them the wherewithal to defend Greece in the Battle of Thermopylae in 480 BCE.

Inherent within the successful Spartan leadership was a commitment to a strong strategic practice, one that had helped Sparta rise as a leader in military warfare.

Strategy of the Spartan Army

Sparta's strategic strength was accumulated over a period of time.

- Right after birth, Spartan boys were prepared for combat service.
- The boys stayed with their families until the age of seven and were then sent to the *agoge* to be trained as soldiers. Here, they were trained physically and mentally and taken in as assets of the state.
- During wars, the council of elders selected the best warriors, who were then approved by the Spartan assembly. The march included mountain-dwelling mercenaries and

---

[2]Formations of the Legion; https://romanmilitary.net/strategy/legform/; accessed on May 2, 2019

cavalry at the front, who carried light weapons. They were also responsible for scouting.
- The hoplites (citizen-soldiers) walked in two long lines and the cargo mules, the slave porters and the noncombatants were positioned strategically on the sides so as to be advantageous to the army.

Each soldier carried his own provisions and weapons, while Helot slaves took charge of their other belongings. The soldiers did not have tents to sleep in at night—they lay on the ground in simple shelters. In the battlefield, the Spartans set up their camp close to a water source. The camp was in the form of a square and had animals, supplies, and slaves placed in the middle.

On the morning of the battle, Spartan hoplites would polish their shields, prepare their weapons, and arrange their long hair. They would also sacrifice a goat to Artemis Agrotera, the goddess of the hunt. Under the watchful eyes of the king, the sages would examine the entrails. This nuanced process was meant to be a symbolically charged ritual.

The Spartans went to war with the Spartan phalanx, a tight military formation consisting of eight men in a row. The formation advanced with music and served as a measure of the Spartan reputation for courage and nerve. The steady rhythm set by the flutes helped the army draw close to enemy lines.

Sparta's army used interesting battle methods. Warriors formed phalanxes and advanced in lockstep with a barrier of shields locked together. Enemies dreaded the colossal damage the phalanxes could inflict.

The Spartans were very restrained even when they won in battle. Instead of exposing the forces to further danger, the army would retrieve the dead. Each Spartan would be carried on their own shields to a burial site near the battlefield. They were then honoured with an epitaph. Other markers were also erected at the site of the battle depending on how significant the battle was.

The strategies of warriors also permeated other cultures across the world. Present day Japanese culture has been traced directly to the ancient martial traditions of the Samurai-dominated culture that ruled the island nation for over 800 years. In his seminal work, *The Japanese Art of War: Understanding the Culture of Strategy*, Thomas Cleary points to the culture of war strategy that has come to influence everyday Japanese life. The reserve and mystery that are deeply rooted in the individual and collective consciousness of the Japanese are derived from their ancient, traditional art of war. There are many interesting facets of strategy that the Japanese deploy in their everyday life, as revealed by Thomas Cleary in his book. An interesting instance of this is how the Japanese learn about their adversaries by engaging them in a discussion where they use superficial content. Strangers from the West may not realize that they are being tested and may often mistake the superficial nature of the interaction for deeper meaning.

Objectives of Strategy

Strategies that manifested in diverse forms across cultures around the world carried specific objectives. Each of these forms was either intended to influence people, groups or communities. The Hindu religious texts such as the Bhagavad Gita offer a compendium of strategies that can be deployed in one's everyday life.

When Arjuna is weighed down by the moral dilemma of having to fight his cousins in the battle of Kurukshetra, Lord Krishna, his charioteer, comes to his rescue. Krishna seized the opportunity to unveil his sermons in the form of a 700-verse

Sanskrit scripture, which he preached to Arjuna. J.A.B. van Buitenen, an authority on the Mahabharat, believed that the Gita was developed to 'bring to a climax and solution the dharmic dilemma of a war.' The life strategies are compiled in the form of 'shlokas' or sermons that carry references to diverse aspects of human lives. Originally documented in Sanskrit, the Gita offers advice for concepts that span the subjects of religion, God, trust, friendship etc.

Ramayana, another popular Hindu religious text, also serves as a compendium of strategic ideas that are woven into the form of a story. The epic is structured and narrated such that every small event in the tale lends a specific pearl of wisdom and insight. Many believe that these lessons would ordinarily have been extremely difficult to circulate, if they were not spun as stories that people could relate to.

Tactics Versus Strategy

The tactician fights the battle and strategists fight the war.

Looking at the very nature of strategy, it is plausible to think that strategy is similar to tactics. In reality, there is considerable difference between the two. Strategy is part of a long-term plan and vision that requires considerable time and effort to be executed successfully. It is because of their long-term objectives that strategies remain flexible and sometimes call for change, if the feedback received warrants a course correction.

A tactician, on the other hand, focuses on the short term and looks for immediate victories. An interesting characteristic of tactics is that once a particular tactic has been deployed, it may not work again. Tactics are usually developed on the fly, as sudden, contextual sets of actions demand immediate relief. This is the reason the strategist ignores particular tactics unless and until a particular tactic impinges on the strategy.

Strategists usually have their eyes fixed on the goal, since the goal is the only trigger that drives them. The path that a strategist chooses goes on to influence the method that tacticians adopt. Usually it is the tactician's ability to execute that strongly influences the accomplishment of goals created by the strategist. In this sense, the distinction between the tactician and the strategist is that between action and planning. However, in almost all situations both the strategy and the tactics employed carry an element of the other. For instance, while the effort spent on planning is strategy-based, the effort devoted to action is tactics-based.

In the military, the tasks related to resource allocation and support systems are left to the strategists, since they are deployed keeping the long-term objectives in mind. The day-to-day positioning of the military fighting units and the way they use arms and ammunition are left to the tactician, who responds according to the context and the ground realities at that point of time. From a militaristic perspective, strategy and tactics are linked to each other through the intermediary—'operations' (Fig. 1.1).

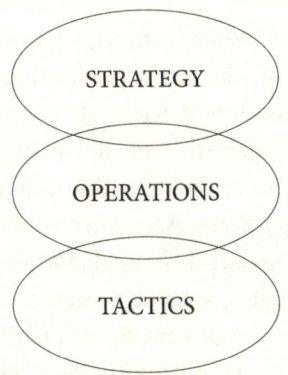

Fig. 1.1: The relationship between strategy and tactics

So it is possible for the strategist to serve as a tactician, but it is rather difficult for the tactician to become a strategist. The one with a macro vision can afford to have a micro vision at times, but the opposite is not true. For example, you can win a battle today by throwing all of your soldiers into action. But this means that the soldiers will be too weak and tired to fight tomorrow's battle against the enemy's reserves. A better option, perhaps, would be to use limited soldiers on the first day, even if it means losing the day's battle—but keep a strong pool of reserves so that the enemy has to do it all over again the next day.

As a practice, strategy operates at two distinct levels. First is at the level of the individual, where strategy requires the deployment of certain types of behaviour that are conducive to being a master strategist or a strategic leader in thought and action. The second level relates to deploying strategy for organizations or entities that exist outside the individual. This is the form of strategy that we see as central to the progress of these entities and their survival in hostile environments.

Changing Forms of Strategy

Over the course of history, strategy has embraced countless dimensions. One of the most interesting characteristics of strategy has been the way it has undergone contextual change. The formats that emerged over the course of the past few centuries are reflective of the transformation in human societies.

During the early Stone Age, when humans discovered fire, the use of strategy was largely limited to achieving everyday tasks such as hunting animals, keeping predators away and more. For these early humans, use of strategy was fairly limited.

Prior to the nineteenth century, the deployment of strategy was mostly seen in wars. This changed with the development of democracies and political systems. We now use strategy both in war and in politics. With the emergence of capitalism, we witnessed another radical shift in strategy. Strategy now came to be deployed for local and global businesses, trade and a diverse set of functions. Today, strategy is primarily used to design and address macro and micro functions of businesses—from business expansion to consolidation strategies, and from marketing strategy to crisis management strategy.

In the twenty-first century, strategy is primarily categorized into two distinct types—emergent strategy and planned strategy. Today, the knowledge economy and the resultant fast-changing technological and business environment call for the deployment of emergent strategies more than planned strategies, since the former allows teams to quickly acclimatize to changing circumstances. Within the realm of emergent strategies, the objective is only to be guided by a clear set of goals and parameters.

The limitations of a planned strategy are obvious. In this type of strategy, the organizational objectives are used to develop a coherent set of business strategies, which can help achieve specific objectives. This type of strategy is now less popular and has limited influence within the bounds of the textbooks. At the same time, there is also an emerging consensus that strategy formulation is a continuous process and calls for the deployment of both emergent and planned strategies.

An alternative to both emergent and planned strategies can be found in the model suggested by Thomas Bayes, an English statistician and philosopher. The eponymous Bayesian method involves guessing the answer and constantly updating the evaluation as the data flows in. The Bayesian process has no certainties—only probabilities that evolve and change in real time. A Bayesian strategy thus starts updating the evaluation from the very first attempt and continues to keep a running score, in order to pinpoint the best alternatives in the complex environment for which the strategy is being designed.

Strategy as Experience and Knowledge

The uniqueness of strategy emerges from its non-replicable nature. We cannot replicate a strategy in the exact same fashion for two different events. It is this uniqueness that makes experiential learning so important in strategy.

Nature has endowed each of us with a mind and a memory that can store experiences. An adult human mind can store millions of experiences. These experiences do not overload our minds, but remain embedded in our heads. They combine together in interesting ways and offer roadmaps for navigating in a particular fashion.

This is why gathering experiences is paramount to training as a strategist. Experiences enhance the stored knowledge in our brains, which in turn drastically enhances our capacity to create effective strategies. When a human mind is brimming with varied experiences, it is not difficult to pick out information at an opportune time for quick deployment.

With strategists delineating themselves as sectoral specialists, these experiences are increasingly microcosmic—and they enable strategists to develop deep vertical competency in the industry sector. Vertical competency enables individuals to strategically connect to customers. A McKinsey report titled *Developing a Customer-experience Vision*, authored by Brooke Boyarsky, Will Enger and Ron Ritter, suggests that successful customer experience strategy begins with an aspiration that is centred on what matters to customers as well as empowering frontline workers to deliver.

The Anatomy of Strategy

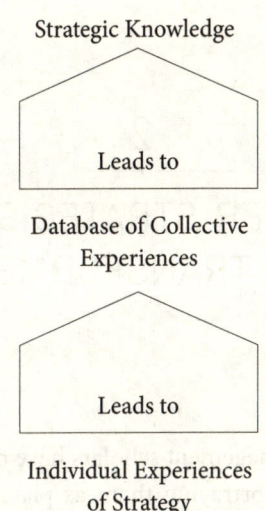

Fig. 1.2: *The Generation of Strategic Knowledge*

When we draw from the learnings of the past, which usually come in the form of experiences, we derive knowledge (Fig. 1.2). Owing to the fact that we go through these experiences ourselves, the knowledge we thus derive is more intense and impactful. In this, our minds simply act as the processors that churn out memory from a collection of distinct and varied experiences and, in so doing, offer us distinctive roadmaps.

2

MASTER STRATEGISTS—
THE TRANSFORMERS

It is ironic that management scholars have reduced the prestige of strategists by portraying them as planners and tacticians. The holistic paraphernalia of strategy have been reduced to functions seeking short-term or near-term solutions, even as their eyes remain fixated on long-term benefits. In the process, the true character of a strategist, as someone who navigates through ambiguity, bias, chaos and complexities to determine alternate courses of action, has been reduced to that of a manager of mundane tasks. It is against this backdrop that the master strategist emerges—like the phoenix that rises from the ashes.

It is therefore important that we try to unravel the true nature, traits and personality of the master strategist. Unless we set clear-cut expectations we may find it difficult to appreciate the true contribution of this potential change manager.

Given the transformative role of master strategists, we can visualize them as individuals who occupy the highest pedestal of leadership. Their position is far above the ordinary strategists we encounter in the everyday, in more ways than one. In most cases, the ordinary strategist functions as a tactician and tries to strategize in the face of quotidian and simple situations (Fig. 2.1).

Master Strategists—The Transformers

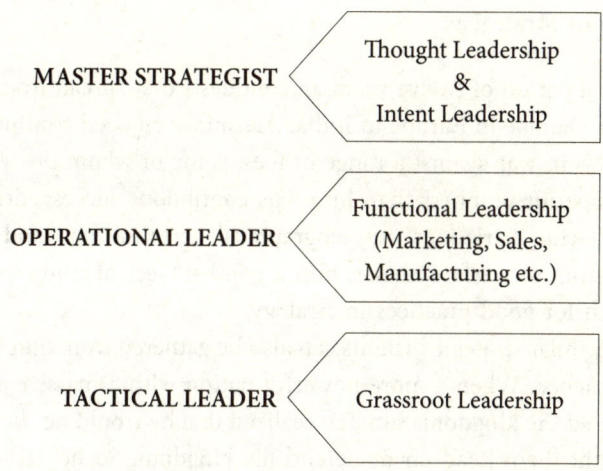

Fig. 2.1: The Hierarchy of Leadership

Master strategists have a much bigger appetite for complexity, and this is how they solidify their positions as tall leaders as they set out to transform the lives of entire communities, countries or regions. Historically speaking, they could be easily seen as generals and political leaders, since only they have the ability to offer this kind of a far-reaching transformation. Today, global corporations embrace master strategists who have begun to influence wider global communities and transform societies in ways that have never been seen before.

The ways in which master strategists have changed are obvious. Going by the classical rendition of strategy, Alexander the Great is considered by many to be one of the greatest master strategists in recorded human history. Though Alexander's strategy was far-removed from modern-day versions, his strategic role remains significant because of his ability to spread out beyond the battlefield. It also included political sagacity and personal traits.

Famous Strategists

Over a period of twelve years, in conquests that spread from the River Danube in Europe to India, Alexander enjoyed continuous success in war against a range of foes, some of whom possessed far superior numbers than him. His continuous success, despite such wide variations in geographical terrain, foes and the spectrum of warfare, makes him a good subject of study in our search for good practices in strategy.

Similar strategic insights can also be gathered from Sun Tzu's experience. When a more powerful nation with a massive army invaded the kingdom, Sun Tzu realized that he would not be able to fight them head on or defend his kingdom. So he deployed a unique strategy. Tzu receded from a direct confrontation and attacked the enemies' homeland, ransacking their villages and cities. This smart strategy compelled his enemies to abandon their plans for invasion and instead focus on protecting their homeland first.

To help us understand the essence of strategy, Sun Tzu postulated that two distinct forces, the Zheng (ordinary) element and the Qi (extraordinary) element, play significant roles. The Zheng element is direct and helps fix the enemy in place, while the Qi element is indirect and unexpected and encircles the enemy, physically and psychologically. When these elements are used together, they help inflict decisive blows on enemies when they do not expect it or are least prepared.

The early part of the twenty-first century saw a reformulation of the character of master strategists. The master strategists that emerged were neither in control of military systems, nor of political ones, but were within arm's length of each. These master strategists were derivatives of a new capitalist world order. Bill Gates, Warren Buffet and Narayana Murthy are the new master strategists, whose global enterprises influence communities, nations and entire regions. As a strategist, Bill Gates is the equivalent of a Winston Churchill or Mahatma Gandhi.

In their structure and influence, modern-day master strategists are not simply limited to the military or politics. They are present across diverse sectors, geographies and forms. Today, some of the most powerful master strategists come from corporates and global businesses and they greatly impact national and continental economies.

Modern master strategists are identified by the broader impact they leave on groups, communities, and nations. This also means that the idea of the modern day master strategist rests on flexibility and agility and they are constantly evaluated and positioned based on their conduct and influence. Today, strategists are also under constant public glare which transforms them into actors who play out their role in the network.

The early part of the twenty-first century has seen the emergence of a new form of organization that has come to dominate out lives. Organizations like Google and Microsoft have emerged as technological behemoths that impact how we lead our lives. Using a series of obvious and not so obvious strategies, these giants have come to occupy a significant part of our lives. In essence, they have moved even beyond that and have gained control of our mental space—mindscapes—in ways that cannot be imagined.

There are many other ways of looking at master strategists. In their functioning, master strategists showcase a strong intent and therefore they can be seen as intent leaders of the highest order. Intent leaders are self-motivated and guided by a higher purpose, which is why they focus on developing and improving capabilities. This is unlike other forms of leadership, where the objectives are steered to achieve parochial goals. Intent strategists, therefore, command vision and authority, which signifies a very robust form of leadership—one that towers above all other forms.

However, it is equally true that the goals that each one of these master strategists nurture are varied and diverse, and far removed from the narrow financial gains or power and politics that ordinary leaders seek.

In democratic setups, many become master strategists by virtue of their positions. The President of the United States, for instance, is the de facto leader of the free world, who is expected to play the role of a master strategist.

The last century has seen the likes of Churchill, Eisenhower and Margaret Thatcher, to name a few, but what allowed them to reach their status were uncertainty and a level of heightened conflict. Unpredictable situations enabled them to use their unique abilities to influence events around the military/political divide.

Nurturing a master strategist depends on extraneous things, such as the presence of systems that provide a favourable environment for the deployment of strategy. Circumstance is perhaps one of the most important determinants of who is seen as a master strategist. It also calls for the presence of support systems that can deploy the strategies. Even a great Greek warrior like Alexander could only achieve his global ambitions because he had at his disposal some of the greatest generals of the time. Closer in time, Microsoft is what it is today because of its executive leadership, that could implement the vision of its founder, Bill Gates.

In this, the master strategists' contribution cannot merely be seen as thought-leadership, but can be measured by their performance, which leaves behind an indelible mark on the pages of history. The master strategist is an individual stripped of all publicity and aura—one who does not exist to manage perceptions, but leaves behind an impact. Perhaps the greatest virtue that master strategists have is the ability to deliver value for the wider good of human civilization. And this, even when there is no visible motive for such initiatives.

We shall now explore some leaders who have stood out in time as exemplary master strategists. Each one of these leaders has left behind a legacy that stands out for its ability to benefit the wider society.

Helmuth von Moltke

Helmuth von Moltke, who was the chief of staff for the Prussian and German armies in the late nineteenth century, is believed to be one of the world's greatest strategists of all time. It was largely due to Moltke's strategies that the several military victories that allowed Otto von Bismarck to assemble the loosely-bound states in Germany into a powerful empire could be realized. Moltke became a superior strategist due to two distinct characteristics.

Firstly, Moltke had the ability to understand the significance of events and not get influenced by such things as current opinion, changing attitudes and his own prejudices. Secondly, he had an extraordinary ability to make quick decisions and take definite action without being deterred by a perceived danger.

It was largely due to the superior strategies of Helmuth von Moltke that Prussia won the Austrian-Prussian War in 1866 and the French-Prussian War in 1871. Though Moltke was a man of action on the field, he was extremely reserved and his directives were largely sent as guidelines to enable independent decision making. The Prussian officers, who were discouraged from making independent decisions in the past, were motivated by Moltke to take individual initiative.

Moltke's idea of strategy is attuned to the very concept of the master strategist we want to imagine. He believed that strategy cannot be learnt or taught, and even if it could be, it would produce mediocre talent. The only progressive idea in disseminating education in its nuanced form, Moltke felt, would be to enable learners to learn and share values based on a common culture which in turn would help them develop their own capabilities.

In devising his strategies, Moltke also believed in learning from experiences of the past and applying them contextually. Moltke closely followed the strategies of both Carl von Clausewitz, a Prussian general and military theorist, and Napoleon Bonaparte, drawing inferences from their ideas. For Moltke, strategy was a very practical art form of adapting means to ends. He also believed in extreme micromanagement and was suspicious of rigid, inflexible strategies; instead he saw strategy as something that can be fashioned and moulded to fit the situation. Moltke also espoused 'Mission Command,' a necessity that was born out of the needs of the nineteenth century. The Mission Command helped the military to be led consistently, and also contained the complexities that cropped up from the challenge of managing the massive army.

Abraham Lincohn and the Transformation of the USA

Abraham Lincoln, the sixteenth President of the United States, was confronted with a tumultuous situation during his tenure. His entry into politics was triggered by the prevalence of slavery and a disintegrating country. Lincoln led the United States through the Civil War, one of the bloodiest periods in its history that heralded the biggest crisis of the nation.

During his presidency, Lincoln was able to initiate the abolishment of slavery by bringing in the 'Emancipation Proclamation', which offered equal rights to blacks. Blacks got the right to serve in the Army and the Navy, which set the pace for the equality that was to unfold over the years.

To achieve his vision, Abraham Lincoln unleashed a multi-pronged approach wherein he combined his administrative ability and political prowess to bring in the desired change. Every step that he took was tempered by the contextual realities of the time.

Lincoln was a self-taught strategist. Despite having no combat experience, he was more strategic than his generals. One of the qualities that made Lincoln a great strategist was his steep learning curve that helped him quickly pick up learning on the job. Though Lincoln had probably never read Clausewitz, his argument was close to what Clausewitz voiced in his treatise *On War*, where war was perceived not as war but as the means to realize the political objective. This perspective placed war not as autonomous, but as an instrument of policy.

Lincoln had to play a more active role in military strategy than any other American president. As General-in-Chief Winfield Scott, the most able soldier at that time in the US, was old and in poor health, Abraham Lincoln was forced to be at the helm of military affairs.

Although Lincoln suffered from setbacks initially he soon learnt the tricks of the trade and adapted to the changing situation. In 1863 Lincoln faced two distinct challenges—reestablishing his control over the army and recapturing public opinion. For this, he made some bold choices, such as getting rid of old beliefs that no longer worked. He also changed his style of leadership and began leading in a different way.

The first thing that Lincoln did was to change the way he

related to his generals. His orders to the generals were now replaced by mild suggestions. But when the mild suggestions were ignored despite repeated attempts, Lincoln quickly reconfigured his stance to a more assertive one. Yet he still retained a unique style of functioning.

In his book, *Lincoln the Unknown*, Dale Carnegie has presented a very interesting analysis of Abraham Lincoln, who had a brilliant strategy for dealing with failure. Using a letter that Lincoln wrote (but never sent) to a General who disobeyed his orders during the Civil War, Carnegie put forth three takeaways from the incident that reflected Lincoln's character. First, Lincoln believed that while delivering feedback, one should think about how it will affect the overall goal. Second, one should always put oneself in the employee's shoes to find the causal factors that may have led him to behave in a certain manner. Consider the pressure they are under before criticizing them. Finally, by not sending the letter, Lincoln found a different outlet for his anger. Finding an outlet for anger will always help the cause and the leader.

To win over the public, Lincoln broke tradition and stepped out of the White House. He successfully used a letter-writing campaign, which improved his connect with the masses. In this, Lincoln was the first president who could develop a new relationship with the military as well as the public.

Lincoln's strong communication skills were an asset that helped him reach out and connect to people. For instance, his speech at Gettysburg in 1864 is hailed as one of the world's finest speeches, which helped Americans gather a completely new perspective while capturing the essence of the American constitution.

Nelson Mandela—the South African Reformist

Nelson Mandela, the South African crusader against colonialism, was a leader who still stands out as one of the world's best. He fought and ended Apartheid. In his struggle against the colonial South African government, Mandela deployed diverse violent and non-violent strategies that came to symbolize the struggle for freedom and equal rights for nations and individuals across the world.

Nelson Mandela was a lawyer by profession. He joined the anti-colonial movement very early in his life. He was particularly appalled by the privilege that white people enjoyed, while the blacks were kept out of the government in their own country. Mandela felt that unless a responsible leadership was set up, it would not help control the feelings of the people. Uncontrolled feelings, he felt, could lead to outbreaks of terrorism that, in turn, could result in bitterness and hostility between different races.

After Mandela joined the South African Communist Party, he supported the strategy of splitting the organization into two parts—a political party and a military wing. The mainstream leadership, however, distanced itself from any military activity. The Umkhonto weSizwe (MK) became a separate and independent organ that was under overall African National Congress (ANC) control but autonomous. The government was warned that if it did not take steps toward constitutional reform and increase political rights, there would be retaliation.

Staying ahead in the movement was very tricky. On the one hand it was important to keep control of the struggle as well as keep the government on its toes. If the ANC would have done nothing then the space would have been usurped by other political parties.

On 16 December 1961, MK began its guerrilla attacks against government installations. The objective was to attack government targets but avoid loss of human life. It was agreed that if these tactics failed, then moving to guerrilla warfare and terrorism would be the next logical step.

Mandela supported a controlled form of violence so that it served political demands. He realized that peaceful initiatives would yield no results, and so he turned towards armed struggle. In his struggle against the regime in South Africa, Mandela did all that he could. He looked at Cuba and the Boer War. He drew lessons and tactics from Jewish fighters against the British in Palestine in the mid-1940s. He also got training from Algerians, from whom he learnt how to use weapons and set off explosives.

He was subsequently arrested in 1962 and sentenced to life imprisonment for conspiring to overthrow the state. In the Rivonia trial that began on 9 October 1963, Mandela and his team were charged with four counts of sabotage and conspiracy. Although they used the trial to highlight their political cause, Mandela and the two other co-accused were sentenced to life imprisonment.

The trial bought an international and a national profile for Mandela. While portraying himself as a victim, he languished in the prison for about twenty-seven years. Over time, he became a reminder of the injustices of the past and also served as a harbinger for an enigmatic future.

His work proved the efficacy of non-violent strategies. Adopting this form of peaceful strategy is self-evident. When we take up violence against a stronger opponent it usually leads to a bloody crackdown with a huge human cost. Moreover, the absence of violence makes it easier to achieve reconciliation. The moral side to non-violence also reflects the pacifist origins of some key proponents.

Mandela's approach to violence in strategy is instructive. He explicitly abandoned non-violence, yet managed to orchestrate a relatively peaceful transition to majority rule in South Africa. Comparing him to Martin Luther King is also instructive. In the late 1950s, both King and Mandela were rising stars in political movements influenced by Gandhi, dedicated to non-violent struggle against racial oppression.

Even inside jail, Mandela did not lose hope. He studied Afrikaans, which became another weapon in his armoury. By 1967, Mandela's status improved and he began having more visitors. He also transformed into a moderate, contrary to his stance when he entered jail. One of the most consistent aspects of Mandela's strategy was his belief in coalitions and his goal of realizing a democratic and non-racial South Africa.

In 1985, Mandela reached an important conclusion while putting up in the new solitary quarters on the ground floor at Pollsmoor. Deploying a remarkable piece of strategic reasoning, Mandela wrote a very compelling letter that is published in his memoir, *Long Walk to Freedom*.

Mandela began by identifying the changed circumstances and the need to identify a renewed purpose. Marking a change from his earlier stance, Mandela put forth the need to begin a discussion with the government. He spelled out that the struggle can only come to a closure through negotiations, as it would help save thousands of lives that would otherwise be lost to conflict. In reversing his earlier stance of armed conflict, Mandela put himself in the firing line and tried to drive home the point that discussions should not be seen as a sign of weakness; rather, as the most logical step forward. Mandela's letter was woven so seamlessly that it sought to give space to both the government and the African National Congress leaders to start thinking of an out-of-the-box solution. The letter helped break the logjam that both the parties had reached.

Mandela's writing is a classic of negotiating strategy, which he wrote using his unique position as someone who could take a lead without seeking the approval of his ANC colleagues. If the government failed, it did not damage the reputation of the ANC, while if it succeeded, it would be good for everyone.

It took almost five years to get to the desired result. In 1985 the South African President, F.W. Botha, offered Mandela freedom in exchange for him renouncing violence. Mandela refused. Despite desiring freedom, he did not fall for this ploy, as he felt that this would mean betraying his principles, leadership and the ANC's long struggle. This decision was a very powerful move and it helped Mandela elevate his position even while drawing global attention to what was seen as an enormously personal sacrifice.

Finally, after his prison term was over, Mandela was released from jail on 11 February, 1990. His party, the ANC, was unbanned by the government. Following this, he began official talks with the government to end white minority rule. In 1991, he was elected the ANC President. Because of the peaceful initiatives, he and President F.W. de Klerk jointly won the Nobel Peace Prize in 1993. Following a multiracial general election in South Africa, Nelson Mandela was elected as South Africa's first democratically elected President on 10 May, 1994. Mandela, however, refused to stand for a second term as president. This was an extraordinary gesture that sealed Mandela's position in the arena of global leadership. Mandela's speech, in which he signaled his pledge to democracy, was watched on television by about a billion people around the world.

Mandela's achievement was extraordinary in several respects. First, he displayed that violence and non-violence can both be used intelligently to achieve the desired objective. The need for violence was limited to the extent that it served as an extra source of pressure on illegitimate governments. Mandela also displayed the virtues of encouraging racial harmony, forgiveness without forgetting, and keeping a strong focus on the future, not the past. As a master of symbolism, Mandela also supported his strategy by being magnanimous towards his former enemies, which made him stand tall. In 1995, for example, Mandela visited the widow of Prime Minister Hendrik Verwoerd, the man who was the main architect of the Apartheid regime and who had put him in prison.

Narasimha Rao—the Father of Indian Liberalization

Sometimes the master strategist includes people who possess the ability to rise to an occasion and deliver value that is least expected of them. This is exactly what happened in 1991 when India achieved its biggest economic transformation after Independence. The architect of this transformation was a seventy-year-old politician, P.V. Narasimha Rao, who, on the verge of retirement, became the Prime Minister of India.

Rao was an active politician throughout his career but many political observers felt that he did not have substantial achievements, both during his stint as a federal cabinet minister and as the Chief Minister of Andhra Pradesh. As Prime Minister from June 1991 to May 1996, Rao oversaw one of the most turbulent phases of India that was also the most transformational. Narasimha Rao rose to the occasion and delivered some of the most extraordinary economic reforms, which are etched as India's watershed moment. Rao's journey is also interesting because it is a riveting tale of how master strategists emerge under unusual circumstances and partake in action that is unexpected of them.

The years that led to Rao's era saw India's foreign debt

skyrocket to $72 billion, which, at that point in time was the third highest in the world. The 'Balance of Payments' crisis touched such dangerous levels that the country had to mortgage around 20 tonnes of gold for $240 million, which kept the economy floating. Rao had inherited a nation that witnessed violent insurgencies, deep economic crisis, and chaos. He lacked majority support and was deeply mistrusted even by leaders of his own political party. But his ability to withstand all these odds helped India to swiftly navigate the turbulent waters and emerge as an economic powerhouse.

Over a period of twenty-one days Rao, along with his handpicked Finance Minister, Manmohan Singh, unveiled a series of reforms that were previously unknown and unheard of in India. Rao used the opportunity to unfurl a series of measures to get rid of old socialist systems that were holding the Indian economy back. Some of his outstanding efforts include liberalizing the Indian economy, framing India's Look East Policy, recognizing Israel, and ending the insurgency in Punjab, amongst others.

Rao used a plethora of talent: his deft skills, political acumen and personality in a transformative and volatile environment where even members of his own party were opposing him in bringing these reforms. Rao used a very interesting strategy to counter these members of the Congress party. For every change he brought about in the economy, he spun an argument that tried to position the new development as an extension of the socialist policies of the previous Prime Ministers from the Gandhi family. Even though Rao was acting against the socialist principles adopted by earlier Congress leaders, he offered such a convincing set of arguments that it was impossible for the members of the Congress to detect the fine print. In his utterances, Rao behaved like a mouse whereas in action, he was a lion.

For his achievements, Narasimha Rao has been hailed as one of the greatest historical figures of all time, on par with leaders like Jawaharlal Nehru, Deng Xiaoping, Franklin D. Roosevelt, Ronald Reagan, Margaret Thatcher and Charles de Gaulle. What made Rao's leadership even more distinct was the fact that even though these great world leaders led a majoritarian government, Rao led a minority government that was hanging by a thread.

Skills of the Master Strategist

Given the wide range of master strategists in today's world, it is difficult to typify the exact nature of a master strategist. For example, organizational functions such as sales, marketing or engineering have clearly defined tasks and competencies. The qualities that master strategists need to possess are varied and diverse.

Nevertheless, there are a set of personal skills and attributes that can be earmarked for all master strategists, across the spectrum:

- *Core Personal Attributes—Courage, Curiosity, Learning Abilities, Patience*

  At the fundamental level, no master strategist can succeed without a set of core attributes. Used in combination, these skills help the strategist to partake in different responsibilities as a thinker and strategic implementer. Courage, for instance, lends a characteristic boldness to the master strategist, who can use it to guide others towards the intended objectives. Curiosity, on the other hand, enables the strategist to be a keen observer—a trait that would come handy in being detail-oriented. Similarly, strategists who possess strong learning

abilities can quickly adapt to new situations and contexts. Strategic thinkers are also endowed with immense patience, which can be a virtue in enabling them to think through a situation meticulously before arriving at a conclusion.

There are many other personal attributes that masters are expected to have, but they are so basic that they are assumed to be inherent. Integrity, for instance, is a virtue that is a given for a strategist. Anyone lacking integrity cannot function as a strategist in the first place, because it would defy the very premise of being a master strategist.

- *Sensitivity—the Ability to Care*
  Strategists are usually looked up to as the ultimate leaders, who drive strategies. This is why it is important for them to remain sensitive to their surroundings. By caring for human constituents, strategists send across a strong symbolic message about their commitment and purpose. This, in turn, helps to nurture the confidence of this constituency, central to the existence of the strategic ecosystem.

- *Analytical and Conceptual*
  Strategists are always evaluated on their ability to be analytical and conceptual. To take strong decisions, strategists should be able to first map their environment minutely and understand the stakes. In this, they learn to navigate through virtual oceans of information that flow in from different sources and churn them to arrive at definite conclusions. This systemic side to strategy mandates that decisions be based on hard facts and a reasoned solution.

  The master strategist should have the skills, knowledge, and attributes needed to quickly assess a situation and gather holistic information on multiple opponents, such as their psychology, wants, needs, strengths, and weaknesses, as well as their physical, emotional, and resource limitations. The master also has to use every bit of knowledge, resources and tricks to maneuver or manipulate them in order to evolve the best possible outcome.

Even while being analytical, the strategist is also required to be creative at the same time. As evident from the design and acceptability of Apple phones or the rebranding of Dubai as a destination for luxury holidays, it is a widely believed fact that the most compelling strategic plans are creative in approach. Being analytical and conceptual at the same time is to be able to embrace the best of both logic and creativity—the limitations of one are countered by the other. Many scholars have proposed the deployment of 'whole brain thinking' to contemplate ideas beyond the logic of the left brain. Developed by Ned Herrmann, whole brain thinking is a theory that focuses on the thinking preferences of different people. Whole brain thinking recognizes the uniqueness of every human brain, which makes it helpful in framing a problem, evaluating an idea or making the best use of critical thinking.

- ***Keeping Focus—Identify Priorities***
  Master strategists realize that the ultimate objective of any efficient strategy is to deliver value in the long-term. This is the reason why it is acceptable to take decisions that may appear unpopular at times. Strategists, therefore, have to resist getting lured by short-term results; instead they must be focused on delivering long-term value.

- ***Detail-Oriented and Discerning***
  Any strategic success requires the strategist to be detail-oriented. The ecosystem for which the strategy is to be deployed consists of many systems, actors, and processes.

And to get the desired results, one should be careful to create strategic plans for every aspect of the strategy. In reality, no strategy can succeed if it is not detailed meticulously. At the same time, the strategist should be discerning. The discerning strategist is able to precisely pin down the elements that can lend a certain advantage to the strategy.

- ***Facilitating Decision-Making***

  In many quarters it is believed that a master strategist who does not enable decision-making at the lower levels of the structure is a sure-shot failure as a strategist. This is because it belies the very foundation of a strategic mindset that is meant to achieve goals through the functioning of a collective.

  Control freak strategists rarely make for good strategists. This is largely because successful strategists see team members as components that can be used to enhance the capabilities of leaders. Like Helmuth von Moltke, efficient strategists enable team members to take localized decisions themselves. For them, the only focus is to keep an eye on decision-making to ensure that the prioritization guidelines align with day-to-day choices.

- ***Managing Complexity***

  The seat of the master strategist hinges on the individual's ability to handle complexity. Complexity management is considered to be the first of all virtues that strategists should have. In fact, it is the ability to manage the sheer span of complexity that defines the stature of a master strategist. Complexity and the stature of a master strategist are directly proportional to one another.

  In any normal situation, the master strategist would confront a bundle of complexities that may relate to such

things as the heterogenous cultural environment, varying experience and abilities of the team, dynamics of the community, structure of the entity being managed, the socio-cultural equations and so on and so forth.

- *Adaptability*

  Adaptability is critical to strategic leadership today. No matter what area master strategists operate in, the speed at which actors and the environment change is simply phenomenal. Being adaptable does not come naturally and requires the strategist to sift through information gathered in real time, or gathered research. Being adaptable requires the strategist to step out of the comfort zone and see things from a fresh perspective. They should be able to seamlessly switch from one area to another by quickly learning the ropes, as and when situations unfold before them.

- *Creating and Sustaining Your Self-Image (Perception Management)*

  At a broader level, master strategists have to also create particular impressions, since impression management is a central component of strategic warfare. Borrowing from the psychological learnings offered by the eminent sociologist Erving Goffman, individuals who desire to create a strong impression on others have to effectively manage their front-stage and backstage. The front-stage represents the image that is visible for the public, while the backstage represents acts or exchanges that remain hidden from the public view. Symbolically, creating impressions of particular kinds enable people to leave specific messages for the group of observers.

Embracing the Grand Strategy

The emergence of the master strategist can also be seen as triggered by the development of the 'grand strategy.' In his book *The Making of Strategy: Rulers, States, and War*, Wiliamson Murray has forwarded three distinct ways in which the traditional idea of strategy has been expanded through the grand strategy.

1. Expanding strategy beyond military means to include diplomatic, financial, economic, informational, and other means.
2. Examining both internal and external forces—taking into account instruments of power as well as the internal policies necessary to implement them.
3. Considering peacetime periods in addition to wartime.

The term 'grand strategy' is derived from academia. It refers to the '…collection of plans and policies that comprise the state's deliberate effort to harness political, military, diplomatic, and economic tools together to advance that state's national interest. Grand strategy is the art of reconciling ends and means. It involves purposive action—what leaders think and want.'[3]

The grand strategy represents a broad, holistic vision of strategy. It includes all the instruments that are available at a state's disposal—diplomatic, intelligence assets, military, and economic. Military strategy is an important element of the grand strategy and this continues even to this day, despite the increasing movement of nations across the world towards a global capitalist economy.

---

[3] Peter Feaver, 'What is grand strategy and why do we need it?' Retrieved from https://foreignpolicy.com/2009/04/08/what-is-grand-strategy-and-why-do-we-need-it/

Despite its immense potential, the grand strategy has been largely limited to the United States of America, which has compelled scholars to question whether it is an American discipline. The only other region outside America where the grand strategy has been explored is the United Kingdom. Elsewhere, it has been completely absent or poorly designed, such as in China, where the grand strategy appeared as a collection of thoughts that was less concerned with the specific attributes of the strategy.

One of the most comprehensive analyses of the grand strategy is visible in the work of John Lewis Gaddis, a preeminent historian and biographer of the Cold War era. Gaddis concedes that grand strategies have traditionally been associated with planning and fighting wars. Drawing from history, Gaddis argues that the grand strategist should prune away emotion, ego and conventional wisdom and should accept that 'if you seek ends beyond your means, then sooner or later you'll have to scale back your ends to fit your means.'[4]

Hal Brands, a professor in the Sanford School of Public Policy and History at Duke University, offers an interesting dimension of the grand strategy that settles it quite effectively. He emphasizes that 'grand strategy' is an ambiguous concept and has no single, universally accepted definition. The term 'grand strategy' was popularized in the mid-twentieth century by the British military historian, Sir Basil Liddell Hart. Subsequent definitions of the concept have been influenced by Hart's insight that grand strategy involves synchronizing means and ends at the highest level of national policy. After this, the concept of grand strategy has been applied to a plethora of items, such as

---

[4]Victor Davis Hanson (2018), 'When to Wage War, and How to Win: A Guide'; Retrieved from https://www.nytimes.com/2018/04/20/books/review/john-lewis-gaddis-on-grand-strategy.html

wartime decision-making or military planning, or to the concept of foreign policy as a whole. It is perhaps for this reason that the grand strategy has not been able to establish itself as a serious area of endeavour.

Applied to organizations, the idea of the grand strategy is perceived differently from the way it is perceived in the political theatre. A discussion on the grand strategy for organizations is taken up in Chapter 5.

The Macro- and Micro-Strategies

For the modern master strategist, it is important to be able to navigate between two distinct worlds—the macro and the micro. The macro offers the holistic view, such as through grand strategies. It is through a deployment of the macro strategy that masters come to know about the society, the environment, and the overall business.

In formulating the macro strategies, the master wants to determine how the system interacts with the environment. Being able to predict the outcome of this interaction is significant if the strategy formulation is to become a success.

However, in its structure, the macro-strategy of a system determines the micro-strategies—the smaller strategies that are deployed to enable a certain macro-strategy. Many would look at the micro-strategy and see it as being the same as tactics, but this may not always be so. Tactics are measures deployed at levels that are even smaller than the micro-strategy (Fig. 2.2).

The micro-strategies are the key to a good macro-strategy because they are like the small components that run an automobile. They are like the braking system, the electrical system, the body of the automobile. The car is only as good as the efficiency of these smaller systems. The strategies that are deployed at the level of these smaller systems, so as to manage the way they function efficiently, are micro-strategies.

Master strategists are usually assessed for their performance through their ability to manage both the micro and macro strategies. This macro-micro relationship also defines a realm that distinguishes ordinary strategists from master strategists. The sheer span of complexity, of navigating to and fro between the local and the global, goes on to define the resilience of individual strategists.

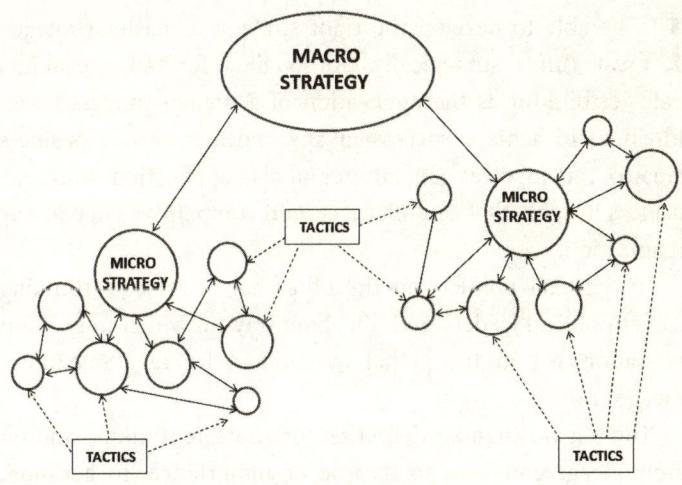

Fig. 2.2: Relationship between Macro- and Micro-Strategy, and Tactics

3
MASTERING STRATEGIC THINKING

To be able to develop the right strategy, a master strategist must think strategically. Although informally speaking, strategic thinking is the application of a mental process by an individual to achieve success in any endeavour, in a business scenario, this involves generation and also application of unique business insights that can offer a certain competitive edge to any organization.

In national politics, on the other hand, strategic thinking enables political leaders to think about ways in which to position the nation within the global milieu and leverage maximum mileage from it.

There is no singular definition for strategic thinking and no common agreement as to its role or importance. In addition, there are no standardized lists of key competencies that define strategic thinking. It is this nebulous character of strategic thinking that makes it such a vague and loosely defined set of skills or techniques.

In his book, *Strategic Thinking: A Comprehensive Guide* (2016), Betz explains that the idea of strategic thinking is based on a philosophy of action that has three postulates:[5]

---

[5] Betz (2016); p1

1. All action is directed to a future.
2. Every action has two intended futures—immediate and distant.
3. Intelligent action is more likely to be productive than unintelligent action.

Developing a Strategic Mindset

1. **Scan the environment to gather data**

   The source environment is the context within which a particular strategy has worked or failed and that we want to emulate. Strategy cannot be thought of in exclusion to the source environment, as it may lead to an error of judgement. The source environment is evaluated by deploying an experience in a particular setting.

   Evaluating the environment is critical to strategic functions at all levels. At the level of an organization, environment scanning is essential to gather accurate information. This way, managers can obtain signals or information from the environment that reflect the advancements, opportunities and conditions around particular situations.

   Effective scanning of the environment is usually the first stage in the process of strategic functioning, and it helps to associate strategy with the environment. The actual tools required for scanning the environment vary widely and depend on the nature of the strategic intent. In the case of organizations, they depend on the size, industry and other factors.

2. **Scanning should be done as per components**

   Scanning the environment is simply not enough. One has to determine the frequency of this environmental scan. This frequency is dependent on the nature of the data and the subject. In developing strategy for organizations, scanning the environment is a tedious exercise and may call for splitting it into smaller parts. The components of environmental scanning can be subdivided into clients, competitors, economic aspects, regulatory aspects, social and cultural aspects, and so forth.

It is not advisable that the tools and mode of gathering the information from the environment be defined through a standardized set of processes. If done, this may reduce or completely eliminate the advantage that one expects to get from the process of strategic planning.

3. **Make decisions**

    Once you have scanned the environment and delineated information into manageable chunks, you should start making decisions. In decision making, you must look at the inter-relationships between different aspects of strategic planning and chose a path that offers the best solution for a given situation. A very effective way to do this is to list out all the possible options and then weigh each one of these against other factors in its area or all other areas that are likely to impinge on it. The Liedtka model of strategic thinking is a powerful model that can help you make effective decisions.

The Liedtka Model of the Elements of Strategic Thinking

In 1998, Jeanne M. Liedtka, an American strategist, developed a model to define strategic thinking as a particular way of thinking and endowed it with a specific and clearly identifiable set of characteristics. The Liedtka model has five elements (Fig. 3.1).

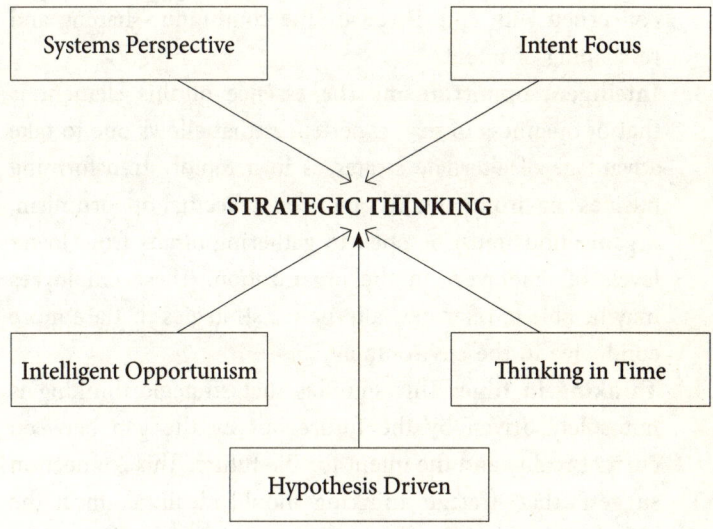

Fig. 3.1: The Elements of Strategic Thinking (The Liedtka Model)

Each of the elements within the model signifies a particular stance:

1. **Systems perspective**: Individuals can use the systems perspective to clarify their role within the larger system. It also helps them to assess the impact of their behaviour on other parts of the system and the final outcome. This approach is the fit between the corporate, businesses, functional levels of strategy and also includes the level of the person.

2. **Intent focus**: The intent focus allows individuals within an organization to leverage their energy and focus their attention for as long as it takes to achieve a goal. In doing so, the individual will have to resist distraction and concentrate for as long as he or she likes. Therefore, strategic thinking is

concerned with and driven by the continuous shaping and re-shaping of intent.
3. **Intelligent opportunism**: The essence of this element is that of openness to new experiences that allows one to take advantage of alternate strategies in a rapidly transforming business environment. To practice intellectual opportunism, organizations must be open to gathering inputs from lower levels of employees in the organization. These employees may be able to offer new alternative strategies that are more conducive to the environment.
4. **Thinking in time**: This signifies that strategic thinking is not solely driven by the future but by the gap between current reality and the intent for the future. This connection suggests that strategic thinking should ideally connect the past, present and future so that the institutional memory and the broad historical context are used as inputs to build the future of an organization.
5. **Hypothesis driven**: Liedtka feels that this approach is foreign to most managers but is an essential component of the strategic thinking process. She feels that in an era characterized by ever-increasing information and decreasing time to think, it is important to develop good hypotheses and test them efficiently. This is important because strategic thinking in essence is hypothesis-driven.

Strategy and the Power of Analogy

Strategy is about choice and robust decision-making. But what is perhaps amazing is the way master strategists go about making these decisions in the face of challenging situations. As a fundamental rule, the quality of thinking determines the quality of the strategy that one is able to decipher.

In a compelling study, Giovanni Gavetti and Jan W. Rivkin, researchers of strategy, have tried to unravel the mind of strategists. They contend that all strategists operate by tapping the power of analogy. Reasoning by analogy unfolds vast amounts of wisdom that can be deployed to arrive at the right strategy.

Analogical reasoning brings about a strong potential for strategic success. Analogical reasoning makes use of the information and the mental processing power of individuals. Here strategists pay attention to select features of the entity for which the strategy is to be created.

The analogical approach can be broken down into two approaches—deduction and the process of trial and error.

Deduction	Trial and error
Definition: Multiple options are weighed and the one that leads to the best outcome is selected.	**Definition:** The learning is gathered after the event or situation, which helps to course correct by formulating a new set of strategies.
Use: Deduction is data intensive and is very effective when used in information-rich settings. For instance, often problems are modular and need to be broken down into smaller parts, deduction works best.	**Use:** It is effective in ambiguous or complex settings where any amount of thinking is bound to fail. For example, often organizational managers have limited cues to see a resemblance to a past experience.

Analogical reasoning has the ability to spark immense creative thinking and help bring about new inroads. This is why business schools use case studies as the mainstay of all global management education. Case studies offer diverse perspectives and enable students to draw lessons that can be applied to their context. Strategists also use case studies wherein they draw lessons from one industry and then apply it to another.

Despite criticism, case studies offer a large repertoire of second-hand experiences that strategists can pick and choose to decide what is important and what is not.

Despite being a powerful and widely used tool, analogies require that they be used widely. Cognitive scientists offer an insight into how analogical reasoning functions. Individuals start with the situation they want to handle (the Target Problem) and relate it to other direct or indirect experiences (Similarity Mapping) to identify the setting that displays similar characteristics (the Source Problem). The solution that emerges from the source (a Candidate Solution) is then applied to the Target Problem (Fig. 3.2).

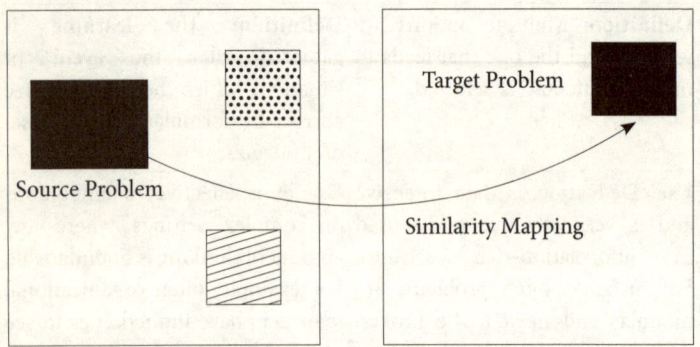

Fig. 3.2: Displays how a solution from an environment is applied to another

Sometimes strategists draw analogies based on superficial similarities. They fail to look at deep causal traits. The failure of Enron Corporation, one of North America's leading energy, commodities and services companies, is believed to have happened due to such bad analogies. In drawing an analogy between the markets for natural gas and broadband, Enron executives failed to nail the deeper differences that existed between these two markets. The last mile capacity that Enron had to deliver in broadband trading was not something that was required for gas wholesalers.

The failure to draw the right analogies and the dangers of focusing on superficial similarities often arise when we deal with problems or situations that are new and unknown. The pioneers of Yahoo, for instance, felt that the portal industry was a media business and therefore they invested more on the company's brand and look and feel rather than the functionality of the search engine.

The inability to draw deep similarities is borrowed from the inherent limitations within strategists. Laboratory experiments conducted by psychologists have revealed that strategy managers always carry with them an idiosyncratic toolkit of possible sources of analogies. These sources of analogies are borrowed from their particular histories and education. Wilbur L. Schramm, a well-known communication theorist and founder of one of America's most reputed writer's workshops, Iowa Writer's Workshop, points to a field of experience that he defines as 'life experiences, attitudes, values, and beliefs that each communicator brings to an interaction and that shape how messages are sent and received'.

This tendency of relying on surface similarity is also worsened by two flaws that are common in how people reach judgments—the Anchoring Effect and the Confirmation Bias.

In the Anchoring Effect, particular ideas or analogies are strongly anchored in management teams. The anchoring effect was effectively demonstrated by Nobel Laureate Daniel Kahneman and his co-author Amos Tversky. They evaluated some experimental subjects by telling them to estimate the percentage of African countries in the membership of the United

Nations. In helping their subjects to make a decision, they used a roulette wheel. The results revealed that the roulette wheel had a strong impact on the final estimates that were presented by the subjects.

The anchoring effect offers strong evidence that early analogies presented in a company can have a lasting influence on employees or external customers. This is particularly true for cases where the decision makers are found to be emotionally attached to their analogies.

The other problem that reinforces the anchoring bias is the 'Confirmation Bias' or the 'Myside Bias' that was first identified by English psychologist Peter Wason in 1960. The confirmation bias refers to the tendency of individuals to either seek information that confirms their particular beliefs or ignore data that is contradictory to their beliefs. There are several psychological studies (Acks, 2018 p15; MacCoun, 1998) that have provided ample evidence that humans are better equipped to confirm their beliefs rather than challenge them, even when there is no compelling reason for them to invest in the beliefs.

Wason showed how people have confirmation bias because they assess the costs of being wrong but do not investigate things in a neutral and scientific way. In an experiment, Wason challenged his subjects to identify a rule applying to series of triples of numbers. He pointed to the three numbers '2-4-6' and suggested that they satisfy the rule. He asked his subjects to find out the rule by constructing other sets of three numbers. For every three numbers, the subjects thought that the experimenter would tell them whether it satisfied the rule or not. This would continue till the time the subject came up with the right rule. Respondents formed rules for the sequence and suggested that they were a sequence of even numbers. In reality, the rule was simply 'increasing numbers'.

Fundamentals of Strategy: The Clausewitzian Perspective

In modern times, the strategies deployed resemble the military strategies of the past, and for a good reason. Although the nature of businesses differs widely from that of war, the original strategies that emerged in the military hold great promise for today's multinational companies.

Carl von Clausewitz was a Prussian general who fought against Napoleon, and wrote *On War*, the most definitive book on the study of warfare. Published in 1832, a year after his death, the ideas shared in the book still reverberate in the corridors of the military and business and is seen as an essential guide for the modern strategist.

The threshold question that is frequently asked by scholars of strategy is, 'Why do we need a strategy in the first place?' Clausewitz offers a simple yet definitive answer to this. He says that strategy should be seen as the necessary response to the inescapable reality of limited resources. Since no entity, irrespective of its size, has unlimited resources, we have to use strategy to make choices about how we can concentrate our limited resources to achieve a competitive advantage. This is the fundamental premise from where strategy begins.

Clausewitz offers an all-encompassing definition of strategy that offers a robust theoretical framework for thinking and acting strategically:

> 'The talent of the strategist is to identify the decisive point and to concentrate everything on it, removing forces from secondary fronts and ignoring lesser objectives.'

In using the word 'identify,' Clausewitz calls for the need to perform a situational analysis in order to develop a deeper understanding of the competitive environment in which we operate and our own realities. He suggests that intelligence always precedes operations.

By using the phrase, 'the decisive point,' Clausewitz refers to the winning proposition, the central idea around which all decisions and activities must be organized so that the competitors can be outperformed. Once the decisive point has been identified, all the focus and determination can be concentrated on it. Similarly, the word 'concentration' points to the pertinent need to bring all our focus to one particular area where we want to make a difference.

In using the phrase 'removing forces,' Clausewitz suggests that the efforts being put in certain other areas that are not part of the current focus or concern should be stopped and these forces should be redirected to the new areas of concern. Finally, the suggestion for 'ignoring' is meant to avoid all distractions and sideshows. These sideshows break the discipline and divert the focus of the team members to other areas, which in turn reduces their efficiency.

Six Lessons from Clausewitz's *On War*

1. **To excel at strategy, first understand what it is**
   Understanding what strategy is all about will set the expectations right. Once we have a well-rounded idea of diverse elements of strategy, such as expected outcomes, key actors, timeline, process etc., we will be empowered to give it our best shot.
2. **Strategy and planning are not the same thing**
   Over the years the distinction between strategy and planning has been so messed up that they are considered to be one and the same. Strategy differs from planning in the sense that strategy is holistic and it is primarily concerned with the

overall purpose and priorities. Strategy's fundamental task is to define a winning proposition behind which all others will rally. Planning relates to execution, that is, we execute the strategy with a plan. So the sequence is strategy first, planning afterwards.

3. **The strength of any strategy lies in its simplicity**

    It is a phrase of old—complexity paralyses, simplicity empowers. All strategies should be written in the simplest possible language so that everyone else in the organization can follow it. Leaders can convey the strategy in interesting ways so that it is understood by others. They can use pictures, examples, messages etc.

4. **Competition is interactive, not static**

    Many strategists nurture the false belief that our competition is standing still and we are the ones who are moving. In reality, competitors are also running as fast as we are and so to close the gap, we must run even faster. Therefore, to steer ahead of competition, it is a good idea to see the world through the eyes of competitors.

5. **Morale makes all the difference**

    According to Clausewitz, if you destroy the morale of the enemy—their will to fight—you have won the war. In business the equivalent of this would be to use the overwhelming power of marketing to drive home the message to your customers that you are simply ahead of your competitors. There are countless companies out there that entered the market with enough brutal force and demeanour to overwhelm the competition, which turned the tables in their favour.

6. **Strategy requires a dynamic process**

    In designing and deploying strategy, it is important that we do not deploy ad-hoc processes. Strategy requires the deployment of a shared process that is inspired by the right kind of thinking. We have to change our perception and deploy the tack to see strategy as learning and not as planning. When we embrace an ability to be adaptive, we are able to realize a competitive advantage that is sustainable.

Decision Making Models

While everyone undertakes decision making in their everyday, the decision making of a strategist stands out for its rigour and methodology. The strategist makes a decision on the basis of a large amount of data, which makes it authentic and impactful.

In many situations, the master strategist seeks information and opinion from diverse sources. Quite often, these pieces of information and opinions may contradict one another. And at times there is also the pertinent need to make a decision quickly. How can a strategist sift through such massive and contradictory pieces of information and take a mature decision? This is surely not very easy.

While you may think that the best way out of this mess is to flip a coin and let chance determine the roadmap, it is not so easy. For relatively simple things the decisions can be easy and quick, but for complex situations and events the choice requires more than common sense. Here are some major decision-making strategies that master strategists can use.

The Single-Feature Model

In this approach you can hinge your decision solely on a single feature. A good example of how to use the single feature is to buy a bar of soap. With a wide variety of options available, you decide to base your decision on the price and go on to buy the cheapest soap available in the store. In doing so, you ignore other features of the product such as the brand, reputation, popularity, scent etc. and focus on a single feature (the price).

You can deploy this model for situations where you are pressed for time and the decision is relatively simple, such as selecting a sales manager for your company. You can decide to give this role to the team member in the sales team who was able to bring in the maximum number of business leads.

The Additive Feature Model

In this model of decision-making you take into account all the important features of the possible choices. You then follow it by systematically evaluating each of these options.

The Additive Feature Model is best when deployed for making complex decisions. For instance, while deciding to buy a car, you can rate a set of features for each car on a numerical scale of 1 to 10. Cars that have these features can be rated 10, while the ones lacking these could be rated 1. After assigning these values to each of these features you can add up the results to determine the car that gets the highest ratings.

This model, though effective in making decisions when faced with a complex set of choices, is extremely time-consuming. It may not be best for strategists who are pressed for time.

The Elimination by Aspects Model

This model was proposed by psychologist Amos Tversky in 1972. In this model, every option is evaluated by looking at one characteristic at a time. The characteristic you select depends on what you feel is the most important. When an item does not meet the criteria you have set, the item is crossed off from your list of options. You continue to do this until all choices are exhausted and you are eventually are left with one option.

Making Decisions in the Face of Uncertainty

While the previous three processes are deployed for cases where decisions are straightforward, we will need to find out the mechanism when there is a certain amount of risk, ambiguity, or uncertainty. We encounter such situations almost every day, where we get stuck choosing between two different tasks—each with its own set of ramifications. In all such cases you will need to weigh both options and figure out the one specific task that you would like to do first.

When making a decision to go with one specific situation and ignoring the other, individuals tend to employ two different decision-making strategies—the availability heuristic and the representativeness heuristic, a rule-of-thumb or a mental shortcut that allows people to make decisions and judgments quickly.

- **The Availability Heuristic:** In trying to find out how likely something is, we usually base our judgement on how easily we can remember similar events that have happened in the past. For example, in trying to determine if you should speed over a particular stretch of the road you are likely to think of the number of times you have seen people getting pulled over by a police officer on that stretch of the highway. If you are not able to think of any examples immediately, you might decide to take a chance. Alternately, if you can recall examples of people getting pulled over, you might decide to just play it safe and drive within the speed limit.
- **The Representativeness Heuristic:** In this mental shortcut you compare your current situation to a prototype of

a particular event or behaviour. For example, if your prototype is that of a careless drunkard who drives his sedan zig-zag and bangs into trees and lamp posts, you might estimate that the probability of your getting a speeding ticket while driving at night is quite low and perhaps almost negligible.

The decision-making process can be simple or complex, and the strategy we use will depend on various factors—including the time we take to make the decision, the complexity of the decision, and the ambiguity involved.

The Building Blocks of Strategy

Even as strategy remains a key driver of organizations, many are baffled by how strategy gets constructed. In a 2013 McKinsey study titled *Mastering the Building Blocks of Strategy*, Chris Bradley, Angus Dawson and Antoine Montard delve deep into this phenomenon to help develop an approach of strategy development that they say is 'thorough, action-oriented, and comfortable with debate and ambiguity.'

Bradley et al. suggest that although good strategy can emerge from a stroke of inspiration or sheer luck, it is possible to develop good strategies by deploying some core building blocks. Their motivation in this approach stems from the fact that strategy development usually consists of hurried efforts that skip the essentials and remain flawed right from the start. They are also wary of strategists who develop partially designed strategies or strategies that remain impractical and are very difficult to practice.

This new method was developed through a study that involved over nine hundred global companies and five years of work.[6] It takes a middle path and views the creation of strategy as a journey and not a project.

The schematic representation of the building blocks of strategy is provided in Figure 3.3. There are five core building blocks that are bookended by two others. The initial block (frame) ensures that the team is able to properly identify and agree to both the questions asked and the decision made when the strategy is developed. The final block (evolve) is meant to suggest the constant monitoring and refreshing of the strategy, with changes in conditions and the availability of new information.

In drawing out these building blocks of strategy, the researchers encountered several interesting challenges and situations. They observed that two-thirds of the two hundred executives they surveyed opined that they always rushed to provide outputs in their strategic-planning processes. They also spoke about their experiences in a financial services company in the Asia-Pacific region that was exploring a growth opportunity involving the creation of an online business. Even as the opportunity appeared lucrative, the members of the strategy team stepped back and spent time thinking through the idea (framing), only to discover that there was a serious risk of cannibalization for one of the existing businesses.

The authors also argued that a focus on strategic building blocks can help organizations develop penetrating insights. Citing complex scenarios, the researchers were able to forward a convincing argument about how these building blocks could be used by the leadership team to collectively unpack complex dynamics to arrive at sharp and accurate diagnosis.

---

[6]'Mastering the building blocks of strategy' by Chris Bradley, Angus Dawson, and Antoine Montard https://www.mckinsey.com/business-functions/strategy-and-corporate-finance/our-insights/mastering-the-building-blocks-of-strategy; October 2013, accessed April 2019

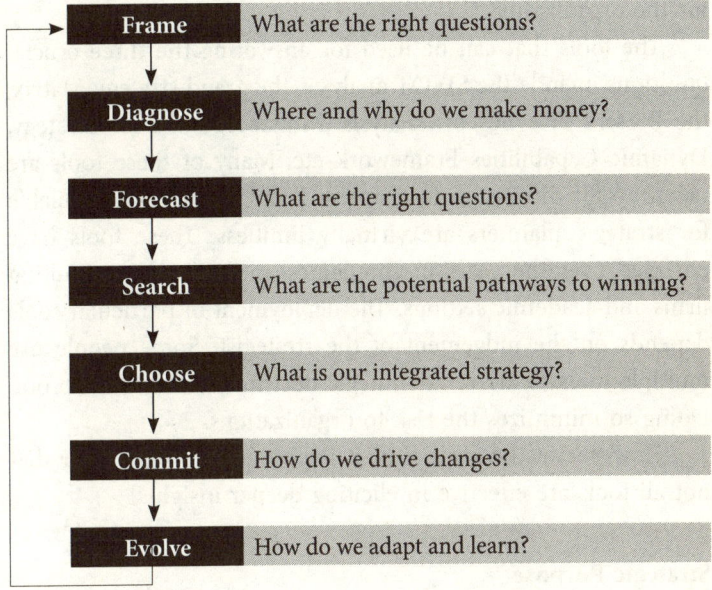

Fig. 3.3: The building blocks of strategy

Components of Strategic Thought and Action

In simplistic terms, all strategic thinking and planning primarily boil down to three questions that one should focus on:

1. Where we are now
2. Where we want to be
3. How we will get there

Many scholars of management believe that if managers are able to answer these three questions in detail, they would have framed the strategic plan for the organization. Each of these three components can be answered by using a multitude of tools or techniques. The bottom-line here is to get a competitive edge for the organization.

The tools that can be used for answering the three crucial questions include the SWOT analysis, the grand strategy Matrix, the Porter's Five Forces Analysis, Mintzberg's 5Ps for Strategy, Dynamic Capabilities Framework etc. Many of these tools are taken up for discussion in chapters 4 and 7. The tools available for strategic planners are virtually limitless. These tools have emerged over the years in companies, management consulting firms and academic settings. The deployment of particular tools depends on the judgement of the strategist. Some people use multiple tools to arrive at strategic decisions that are fail-proof. Doing so minimizes the risk to organizations.

However, at the same time it is pertinent to remember that not all tools are effective in eliciting deeper insights.

Strategic Purpose

Any organization that exists in the world today needs to specifically answer the question: 'what is your strategic purpose?' The strategic purpose pretty much defines the identity of an organization.

Employees, customers, shareholders and institutional actors all want to ascertain that organizations have a strong purpose for existing in the market. Without clarity around the shared purpose, an organization tend to give out a very shaky message about itself. When companies do not have a clearly delineated strategic purpose they negate many things—marketing efforts, websites, sales collaterals and employees.

Defining a clear purpose for the organization is at the core of a strategist's job. In the absence of a strategic purpose, the organization and its strategy become a mystery. And this has a direct bearing on its very existence.

The strategic purpose is expressed by three distinct elements—the Vision, the Mission, and Values. Each of these elements has a definite role in the objective to convey the organization's strategic purpose.

The Vision Statement: The vision statement is concerned with the desired future state of an organization. In formulating the vision statement, managers ask questions like, 'If we are sitting here in thirty years what would we want to have created or achieved?' A typical vision statement would be something like, 'To be the world's leading automotive brand.'

The Mission Statement: Mission statements have a long-term purpose and provide employees and other stakeholders with clarity regarding the overriding purpose of the organization. In developing the mission statement, strategists should begin by asking questions like, 'Why does the organization exist?' and 'How do we make a difference?'

Values: Values communicate the underlying and enduring core principles that guide an organization's strategy. In designing these corporate values managers should ask questions like, 'Are these values going to change with circumstances?' If the answer is yes, then the values do not qualify to be labeled as 'core' and 'enduring.' According to Peter Drucker, a management theorist, 'Culture eats strategy for breakfast.' This signifies the interrelationships between culture and values. Values usually form the basis for strengthening team interaction and culture.

Strategic Planning

Strategic planning is referred to as the organization's process of defining its strategy, or direction, and is also used to make decisions on the allocation of resources. Strategic planning emerged in the 1960s and it remains an important aspect of organizational management. Organizations use strategic planning to set priorities, strengthen operations, ensure that stakeholders are working towards common goals, and focus energies. Put differently, strategic planning can be seen as a disciplined effort at making fundamental decisions and actions, which determine what an organization does, with a focus on the future.

As mentioned before, strategy is primarily of two types, planned strategy and emergent strategy. Strategy planning helps us to address the need for the first type. It is analytical in nature and helps in synthesis. This means that it helps to find the dots (formulation) and also to connect these dots (implementation). This is why strategic planning happens around the formulating stage.

As a process, strategic planning includes inputs, outputs, activities, and outcomes. It may be formal or informal and typically has an iterative nature with feedback loops built into the process. When we deploy strategic planning, we are able to gather elements that can provide inputs for strategic thinking. Strategic thinking serves as the actual guide for strategy formation.

Typically, the strategic planning process consists of five broad areas (Fig.3.4). Each of these parts is a relatively large area of endeavour and has independent processes.

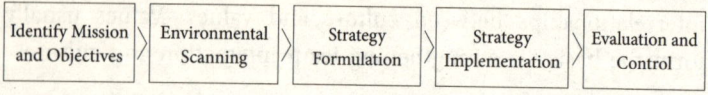

Fig. 3.4: The broad areas of the strategic planning process

Dealing with People

For all strategists the focus is primarily on dealing with humans. It is therefore important to gather some fundamental psychological theories that will enable you to deal with people effectively. There are hundreds of theories that relate to humans and the relation they share with others. One of the most important theories that relates to strategy is Cognitive Bias.

Cognitive Bias

A cognitive bias refers to a systematic pattern in which individuals tend to deviate from the norm or rationality while judging others. Here individuals develop a social reality that is based on their own subjective perception. This 'manufactured' social reality is not objective and it defines their behaviour in the social world. Eventually such cognitive biases usually lead to perceptual distortion, inaccurate judgment, illogical interpretation, or irrationality.

Many of these biases are related to memory or problems related to attention. Since attention is a very limited resource, individuals are compelled to be selective with the things around them. This in turn forces subtle biases to emerge that greatly influence the way in which people look at the world around them. Some cognitive biases emerge as a by-product of human processing limitations such as absence of appropriate mental mechanisms (known as bounded rationality) or a limited capacity for information processing.

However, despite its negative influence on our lives, not all cognitive biases are bad. Many of these biases help individuals to adapt to their surroundings and make quick mental decisions. They offer mental shortcuts and cues that can help individuals navigate out of a tricky situation, such as when people are walking down a dark stretch of the road with the presence of drug addicts or muggers.

Over the past several decades, research has helped build an extensive list of cognitive biases. These biases, identified by psychologists Daniel Kahneman and Amos Tversky in 1972[7], have practical implications in diverse areas such as clinical judgement, finance, management and entrepreneurship.

The nine most common types of cognitive biases that can influence human thinking:

1. **Availability Heuristic**: This bias refers to the tendency of placing greater value on information that comes to our mind quickly. With this, humans tend to overestimate the recurrence of similar things taking place in the future.
2. **Confirmation Bias**: This bias refers to the favouring of information that conforms to existing beliefs and discounting the beliefs that do not conform to these individual beliefs.
3. **Halo Effect**: The Halo Effect is a bias that emanates from the overall impression of a person and the way we think and feel about their character. This usually applies to the physical attractiveness of individuals which compels us to rate their other qualities.
4. **Self-Serving Bias**: This bias borrows from the tendency of blaming external forces when bad things happen to us while giving ourselves the credit when good things happen to us.
5. **Attentional Bias**: A tendency to pay selective attention to certain things while ignoring others.
6. **Actor-Observer Bias**: This relates to the tendency of

---

[7]Kahneman, Daniel and Tversky, Amos, Subjective Probability: A Judgment of Representativeness, *Cognitive Psychology, 1972*, Accessed May 2, 2019

attributing our own actions to external causes and attributing the behaviour of other people to internal causes. For example, we may attribute our own high cholesterol to genetics while blaming others with high levels of cholesterol for lack of exercise and poor diet.

7. **Functional Fixedness**: This refers to the tendency of seeing objects as working in a particular way. For instance, we may have a tendency to imagine the role of a personal assistant as being that of support and not of leadership.
8. **Misinformation Effect**: This refers to the tendency of post-event information to interfere with the memory of the original event.
9. **Optimism Bias**: In this type of bias, we have a tendency to believe that we are less likely to suffer from misfortune and more likely to attain success than our peers.

This is not an exhaustive list and there could be many other psychological theories of human behaviour. You may learn about this by picking up any good book on behavioural psychology.

4
DEPLOYING STRATEGIES IN CORPORATE ORGANIZATIONS

Strategies are central to the existence of global corporates today. It is only with well-designed strategies that organizations steer ahead to become market leaders. No wonder this is why corporates have become the new battleground for master strategists.

Though the strategy deployed in organizations can be of many types, we can broadly split it into four distinct areas, in terms of the hierarchy (Fig. 4.1). The areas are listed below in descending hierarchical order:

1. **Corporate Strategy**: This describes the organization's overall direction towards growth. The corporate strategy helps to develop a strategic roadmap at the highest level for organizations.
2. **Business Strategy**: This relates to the business unit level or the product level and emphasizes the overall improvement of a firm's products or services in an industry or geographical area.
3. **Functional Strategy**: This type of strategy is taken up in a specific functional area. Here the emphasis is on achieving the objectives laid out in the corporate and business levels

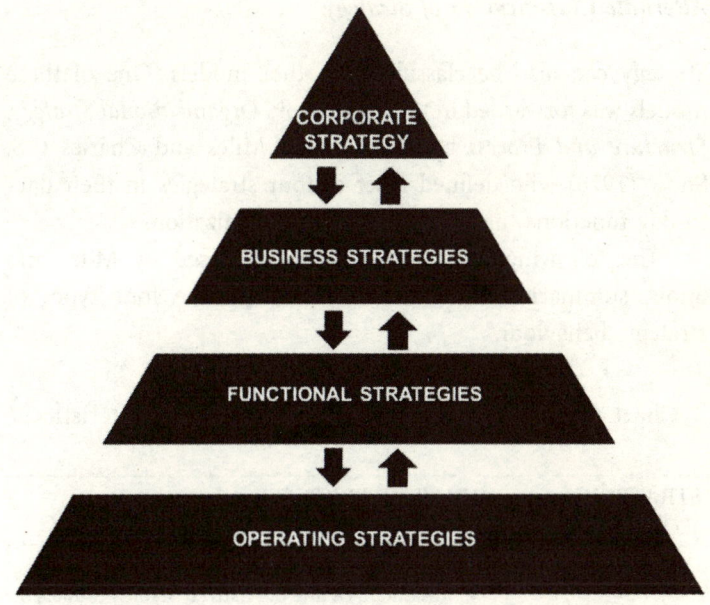

Fig. 4.1: The Hierarchy of Strategy in an Organization

by maximizing resource productivity. The key focus here is to develop and nurture a distinct competence that can offer a competitive edge to the organization.

4. **Operating Strategy**: This type of strategy seeks to examine how organizational components (resources, processes, and people) help deliver the corporate, business and functional level strategies.

Scholars (Alkhafaji, 2003) have suggested a fifth category, the enterprise strategy, which sits at the top, above the corporate strategy. The enterprise strategy is the overall strategy and it characteristically combines all the other strategies.

Alternate Classification of Strategy

Strategy can also be classified by other models. One of these models was forwarded in the book book, *Organizational Strategy, Structure and Process* by Raymond E. Miles and Charles C.S. Snow (1978) who defined a set of four strategies in their day-to-day functions that are deployed to organizations.

The following chart (Chart 4.1), proposed by Miles and Snow, summarizes the characteristics of these four types of strategic behaviour.

Chart 4.1—Strategic Typologies and their Characteristics

STRATEGIC TYPOLOGY	CHARACTERISTICS
Defender Strategy	A company that follows this type of strategy: • Maintains a line of relatively stable products or services and has a tight control over product and market. • Does not tend to search for new opportunities beyond its domain. • Has managers who are highly specialized in their area of work. • Has centralized control and decision making. • Ensures strategic actions are geared towards gaining market share based on the offer of better quality products, improved services and/or lower prices.
Prospector Strategy	A company that follows this strategy: • Seeks new business opportunities aiming to continuously increase its line of products/services. • Has managers who are highly flexible regarding change and innovation. • Has decentralized business activities.

Analyzer Strategy	A company that follows this strategy: • Aims to keep a relatively limited line of products/services stable while it tries to add one or more product(s)/service(s) that were successful in other companies in the same industry. • Protects its stable market share. • Has centralized control and decision making; however, it is possible to identify flexibility in its actions.
Reactor Strategy	A company that follows this strategy: • Is not qualified to effectively respond to the implications of changes that take place in the environment. • Does not take risks with new products/services unless it is threatened by competitors. • Has highly centralized control and decision-making. • Has rigid organization structure.

Source: Miles and Snow (1978)

Master Strategists in Corporates

With market driven economies dominating much of the world, organizations and governments are trying to deploy strategists to drive all aspects of their functioning. Hence, a master strategist has come to be known as the turnaround expert, the innovation manager, and also the operational excellence manager.

These strategists, notwithstanding their designation, usually focus on broader aspects of the organization. Using a wider repertoire of strategic tools and competencies, these strategists break the corporate strategies into smaller micro-level strategies to be managed by individual functions (Human Resources, Marketing, Engineering etc.).

American economist and Harvard Professor, Cynthia A. Montgomery, offers a compelling insight into the value strategic leaders can bring to their organizations. For her, the leader and the strategist are linked inextricably. In an article published in McKinsey in 2012,[8] she proposed that in organizations, strategy has to undergo a certain realignment of sorts, broadly centered on the following themes:

1. *The strategist as meaning maker*
   It is important to realize that there is a crucial link between a leader and the strategist. This is because the leader is the strategist who creates meaning for organizations by determining its very identity. In this sense the leader and the strategist should not be seen as two distinct roles but one that is a fusion of the two.

2. *The strategist as voice of reason*
   In a marketplace that is extremely crowded, as each organization competes to grab the customer's dollar, there are organizations that take the competition positively. Even though the market forces are beyond the control of most companies, strategists understand that competitive forces determine the company's performance. This is why the leader-strategist deploys the voice of reason by recognizing competition and then starting to lay their plans.

3. *The strategist as operator*
   Good strategy is not a far-fetched idea but is the bridge that connects the economics of the market, the core business ideas, and action. This bridge is founded on clarity and realism and calls for real operating sensibility. A good

---

[8]Montgomery, Cynthia A, 'How strategists lead', Published on www.mckinsey.com https://www.mckinsey.com/business-functions/strategy-and-corporate-finance/our-insights/how-strategists-lead

example of this can be gathered from the example of the Italian brand, Gucci. When the Gucci Group hired De Sole, a tax attorney to lead it in 1995, after years of poor sales and mounting losses, he deployed an interesting strategy. De Sole summoned every Gucci manager to Florence and sought their responses on what was selling and what was not. In doing so De Sole tried to resolve the business problem with data rather than philosophy. What followed was a series of steps that went on to revive the company and proved that companies can deliver on promises if its strategists think like operators.

4. *A never-ending task*

    Maintaining strategic momentum requires consistent efforts, that are ongoing and involve making multiple choices over time. Leaders evaluate the needs to overhaul the organization's strategy in dramatic ways. These changes help nurture new ways of thinking and also inspire and serve as catalysts for organizational growth.

Deploying the Grand Strategy

Master strategists who operate in the corporate world are required to handle the 'grand strategy'. Also called 'Master Strategy' or 'Corporate Strategy,' grand strategy describes multi-tiered strategies and also introduces strategic thinking at the level of corporations. Businesses use 'grand strategy' as a general term to depict a broad statement of strategic action that seeks to achieve long-term objectives.

Today organizations are widely deploying the grand strategy to create feasible strategies. However, despite its potential, the grand strategy should not be seen as a replacement for other forms of analysis and assessments such as Strengths, Weaknesses,

Opportunities and Threats (SWOT) analysis, Strategic Position & ACtion Evaluation (SPACE) Matrix, and the Boston Consulting Group (BCG) Matrix.

The Grand Strategy Matrix

All organizations can be positioned in one of the four quadrants of the Grand Strategic Matrix. This matrix is based on two dimensions—competitive position and market growth. Figure 4.2 displays the components inside the Grand Strategic Matrix.

Fig. 4.2: The Grand Strategy Matrix

Explanation of the quadrants:

Quadrant 1 (Strong Competitive Position and Rapid Market Growth)	Companies that are placed in the Quadrant 1 of the grand strategy Matrix are considered to be in the best strategic position. This is the quadrant where companies have a strong competitive base and they operate in very fast-moving growth markets. The position of these firms enables them to adopt strategies such as market development, market penetration, product development etc. The objective behind choosing these strategies is to focus and make the current competitive base stronger.
Quadrant 2 (Weak Competitive Position and Rapid Market Growth)	Companies located in this quadrant are in a tricky situation and they should evaluate their current approach to the market. Even when their industry is growing these firms are not able to compete effectively. This is exactly why the firms have to find out why the current approach is ineffective and what measures can be adopted to improve its competitiveness. The firms in this space can adopt horizontal integration, divestiture, liquidation etc.
Quadrant 3 (Weak Competitive Position and Slow Market Growth)	Firms situated in Quadrant 3 operate in slow-growth industries and have weak competitive positions. To survive, it is essential for these companies to make certain drastic changes so as to arrest further demise and possible liquidation. The companies here will have to undergo extensive cost and asset reduction. They can also choose alternate strategies such as shifting resources away from the current business into different areas. If all these measure fail, the companies may have to go for divestiture or retrenchment.

Quadrant 4 (Strong Competitive Position and Slow Market Growth)	Companies positioned in Quadrant 4 are in a slow-growth industry but have strong competitive position. These organizations should go for integration in related or unrelated areas so as to widen and create a vast market for their products and services. These companies can also diversify into more promising growth areas. They can also enter into joint ventures.

It is evident that **Quadrant 1** is the most promising quadrant for companies and it is here that all organizations want to be situated. Companies located in the other three quadrants, however, have to function with agility and undertake measures so that they are able to improve their positions.

While the grand strategy Matrix may not be the only method to decipher and resolve the competitive positioning of organizations, it is one of the most versatile strategies available. The grand strategy Matrix is also advantageous because of its objectivity and ability to convey a lot of information in a simplified format.

The SWOT Matrix

Another interesting matrix that is popular and widely used in evaluating organizational strategy is the SWOT Matrix. SWOT analysis was developed at the Stanford Research Institute between 1960–1970, as a project initiated to develop a better method for strategic planning.

A SWOT Matrix consists of four individual quadrants, each representing the organization's strengths, weaknesses, opportunities and threats, in that order. However, it is worthwhile to remember that while calculating the Strength and Weakness we will only focus on the internal factors. Similarly the Opportunities and Threats will be calculated against external factors. Figure 4.3 provides a schematic representation of this matrix of an imaginary organization.

	HELPFUL	HARMFUL
INTERNAL FACTORS	**STRENGTHS** • Strong quality team • Flat hierarchy in the organization • Strong processes • World-class engineering team • Highly motivated employees (as gathered fro racent surveys)	**WEAKNESSES** • High workloads • Experience missing in some areas • Not well-connected with political establishments • Very few people in the senior management team who can become brand ambassadors • High • High
EXTERNAL FACTORS	**OPPORTUNITIES** • Unserved markets for specific products • Fewer competitors • Positive press coverage of products in the past one year • World-class engineering team • Employees are highly motivated (as gathered from recent surveys)	**THREATS** • Emerging competitors with VC funcing • Changing regulatory environment • Changing customer attitude towards the company • Dipping motivation of employees

Fig. 4.3: The SWOT Matrix drawn for an imaginary company

The SWOT Matrix helps managers to interpret the best strategic options for their business from a multitude of choices that are placed within the external environment of its opportunities and threats.

Practitioners of both the grand strategy Matrix and the SWOT Matrix offer distinct insights into the organization. By combining these two tools, master strategists can gather a much deeper insight on the organization's standing. The patterns and trends that these two matrices collectively provide the strategist, greatly enhance the quality of the organization's strategy.

The Balanced Scorecard

Modern organizations also use another strategy management framework to aid strategic decision making—the Balanced Scorecard (BSC). It is a strategy map where organizational strategy can be placed in a simplistic language so that everyone can understand it. This simplicity of the BSC is perhaps the one essence that has helped it to emerge as a widely-used strategy mapping tool. The BSC was first introduced by Harvard academic Dr. Robert Kaplan and theorist Dr. David Norton and was first published in 1992 in their *Harvard Business Review* article titled 'Using the Balanced Scorecard as a Strategic Management System'.

The Balanced Scorecard helps managers to navigate to future competitive success. It provides an accurate understanding of organizational goals and the methods for realizing these. The BSC translates the organization's mission and strategy into a comprehensive set of performance measures that can be easily managed.

The BSC measures organizational performance across four balanced perspectives—Financial, Customer/Stakeholder, Internal Process, and Organizational Capacity (originally called Learning and Growth). Figure 4.4 is a tentative representation of the Balanced Scorecard. However, it is important to remember that the structure of the BSC does not make a difference and the only criterion is to undertake an analysis of the four distinct areas of businesses.

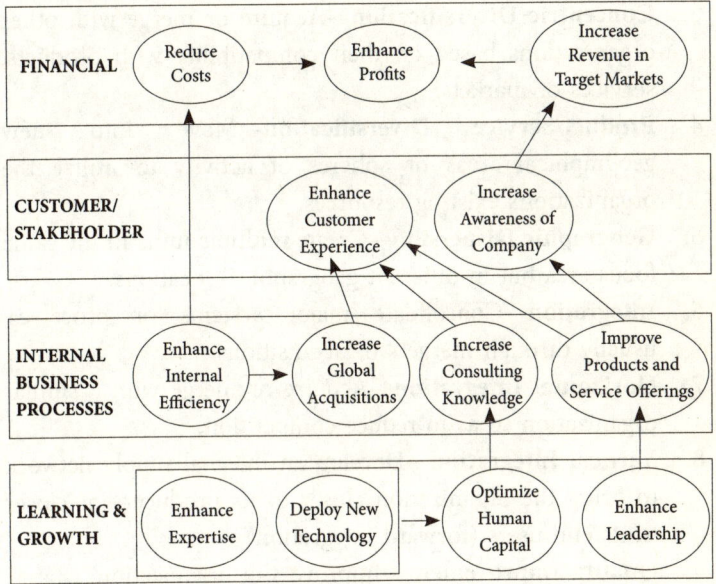

Fig. 4.4: Sample of the Balanced Scorecard for an imaginary organization

Twenty Examples of Organizational Grand Strategy

Organizational grand strategies represent a broad canvas of strategic intervention. They can be short-term and focused or long-term and far-reaching. Successful organizations review widely used grand strategies before deciding to position themselves. Following is a list of about twenty grand strategies that may be deployed by organizations, to realize the desired objective:

1. **General Growth**—Grow the size of the organization to realize economy of scale and widen the organization's marketplace.
2. **Concentrated Growth**—Increase the market penetration of a limited number of successful products or services.

3. **Concentric Diversification**—Acquire or merge with other organizations based on their compatibility with products, services or markets.
4. **Product/Service Diversification**—Move into new geographical areas or spheres of activity to utilize the organization's existing resources.
5. **Geographic Dispersion**—Create multiple units in the same focus area but in different geographical locations.
6. **Integration**—Consolidate major systems or processes, usually through mergers or acquisitions.
7. **Horizontal Integration**—Acquire or merge with a similar organization so as to reduce competition.
8. **Vertical Integration**—Develop an internal supply network to bring the organization closer to its producers or closer to its end users (forward integration).
9. **Quality Improvement**—Improve the organization's status, capacity, resources and influence through continuous up-gradation of its existing products and services etc.
10. **Brand Enhancement**—Deploy powerful creative marketing strategies and sustain them over a period of time.
11. **Market Development**—Add new customers in specific markets using renewed strategies.
12. **Product/Service Development**—Create new, but related products or services that can be sold to existing primary markets.
13. **Focus/Specialization**—Limit and focus the organization's activities by withdrawing from certain areas of focus or activity.
14. **Innovation**—Create products or services that are perceived to be new in the marketplace by applying cutting-edge information technology.
15. **Operational Excellence**—Select cost-and-convenience

leadership by offering products/services with the lowest cost and ready accessibility.
16. **Strategic Alliance**—Develop teams, partnerships, joint ventures, shared services or cooperative programmes with suppliers, customers or compatible enterprises so as to develop new products, services or markets.
17. **Financial Independence**—Strive to diversify the organization's funding sources to gain control over its fiscal environment.
18. **Downsizing**—Reduce the scope or scale of products and services to fit financial or other constraints.
19. **Divestiture**—Sell off or shut down a segment of the organization.
20. **Liquidation**—Go out of business if the organization is no longer viable, usually by selling off the organization for its tangible assets.

Decision Scientist—the Modern Avatar of the Master Strategist

An excessive emphasis on organizational strategy has seen the emergence of a new kind of professionals—the decision scientists. Decision scientists are equipped with interdisciplinary knowledge and their singular objective is to enable better decisions. Decision scientists work best when business problems are not adequately defined and where the factors affecting a problem are not obvious or inadequately understood.

Decision scientists do not base their judgement on intuition or the traditional trial and error methods; rather, they use a wide variety of interdisciplinary knowledge to make solid decisions. Decision science includes such things as decision analysis, risk analysis, cost-benefit analysis, cost-effectiveness analysis, simulation modeling, and behavioural analysis. It also includes operations research, microeconomics, statistical inference, cognitive and social psychology, and computer science.

The decision scientist is different from a data scientist, although the difference is subtle. The data scientist finds meaning by churning big data while a decision scientist looks at big data with the objective of solving a business problem. The difference is that of orientation. To articulate differently, while a data scientist develops a framework for a machine to make decisions, the decision scientist develops a framework for humans to make decisions.

However, despite such advancement, questions abound. Why do we need data scientists when traditional strategists are able to provide considerable insight on businesses? The answer to this lies in the massive amounts of data that flows with great speed, making it virtually impossible for ordinary humans to decipher meaning from it. An enhanced speed of data flows also means that the businesses have to take quick decisions. Thus by enabling faster business and strategic decisions, decision science helps enhance the capabilities of leaders manifold.

However, businesses today need a fine mix of both data science and decision science. And this is not without reason. Excessively focus on data science brings in issues related to decision science. On the contrary, if organizations excessively focus on decision scientists without investing in data science, decision scientists are rendered ineffective. A decision scientist is just as good as the data that is made available to them.

For master strategists, decision science can serve as a powerful enabler for their day-to-day functioning. It can enable them to sift through massive volumes of complex data and use these as powerful scenario-generation engines to identify risks, rewards and uncertainties.

5

DESIGN THINKING AND STRATEGIC DESIGN THINKING

As we set out to explore ways of thinking about strategy, we encounter two crucial areas that facilitate strategy formulation. These concepts are Design Thinking and Strategic Design Thinking. While these concepts may appear to be the same, they are endowed with subtle differences.

Design thinking signifies 'thinking by doing,' as opposed to traditional strategy where the analysis and planning is done first, before the actual project is implemented. It is for this very reason that traditional strategy is seen as mired in 'overthinking' which many see as 'death by analysis.'

Expressed differently, design thinking is all about applying the principles of design to other areas of decision making. Here creative and critical thinking are combined to organize information and ideas, make decisions, improve situations and develop knowledge and insights. The ultimate mindset in design thinking is to focus on solutions and not only on the problem (Fig. 5.1).

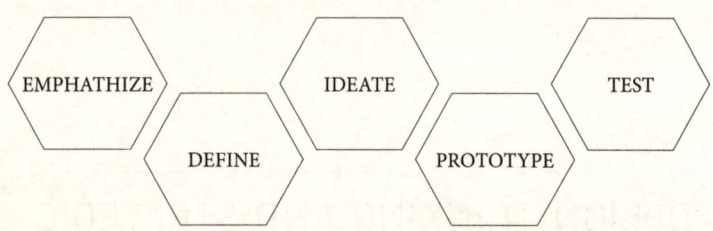

Fig. 5.1: Steps in the Design Thinking Process

Design thinking has tremendous implications for the corporate world. Since design thinking focuses on iteration and real-world experiential learning it helps infuse a design-driven culture in organizations. Businesses use design thinking to reduce expenses and enhance the speed to market. It also focuses on the customer and tries to resolve their issues. Design thinking can be applied to anything—products, services, and processes. This is why it is deployed by global giants like Google and Apple in their day-to-day operations. The concept can be applied equally well in smaller companies.

There are certain key mindsets that govern the concept of design thinking. These mindsets are the heart and soul of design thinking and are inherent to all design thinking initiatives.

Foresight	While coming up with new ideas try to innovate on the basis of the future you envisage.
Getting Inspired	Surround yourself with people, places or things that inspire you.
Feedback Driven	Gather the feedback on your product or idea by studying your target.
Learning by Doing	Instead of thinking and guessing, get down to doing it.

Head to Hands	When ideas come to your head do not let them go away; instead, try to work them out by sketching, discussing, prototyping.
Visualization	Use visualization to communicate your ideas, problems and solutions.
Appreciating Negative Result	Try to take failure in your stride by thinking of the learning that you gathered in the process.

Design thinking can use a wide variety of tools to focus on iterative development such as structured brainstorming, mind mapping, journey mapping, value chain analysis, assumption testing, rapid prototyping, storytelling, etc. The development of computer-based technology has seen a proliferation of hundreds of design thinking tools. Some of the most popular tools include Typeform, Zoom, Smaply, SessionLab, etc.

The Goal of Design Thinking

The objective of design thinking is to identify an innovative solution to a problem. The solution should ideally satisfy three criteria:

1. **Desirability**: Thinking about what customers need, by stepping into their shoes.
2. **Feasibility**: Use observation to identify themes and models with the objective of building relationships and gathering deeper insights on the behaviour of customers.
3. **Viability**: Identify the ultimate winning solution by evaluating it in terms of profitability and sustainability.

Strategic Design Thinking

When design thinking is applied for strategies and innovation within an organization it is known as Strategic Design Thinking. Design thinking now lies at the core of effective strategy development and organizational growth and competitiveness.

Strategic Design Thinking helps translate insights into actionable solutions, provide new ways for organizations to position products and services, and transform the opinion of stakeholders. This design model is also crucial to the organizations' success in changing, unpredictable markets.

Master strategists who operate in the corporate world understand the immense possibilities of deploying strategic thinking for developing strategies. Today they deploy strategic thinking to conceive and create value-added products and services, build product/service differentiation, build customer loyalty, design total brand experiences, shape the internal culture of organizations, prototype, visualize etc.

In the 1980s and 90s, Sony was one of the earliest companies that made effective use of design at the tactical level. Even though design was not present as a part of the company's visions and missions, the product team embraced design to bring about a competitive edge to the company. The team used design to develop outstanding products like the Sony Walkman and PlayStation that became instantly popular. In the process the design team earned a strong reputation in the company and came to be valued even more. The team was given the opportunity to engage with the top management officials and present visions of the future. This interaction indirectly and purposefully influenced Sony's future innovation plans.

British Airways was another company that also made use of strategic design thinking in the late 1990s. The airlines used design to manage and strengthen its leadership position. Its design-led initiatives such as the world's first fully flat beds in First Class and later in the Business Class, were experiences that portrayed its progressive thinking and raised the standard of traveler experiences.

The design focus was also enhanced by the initiatives of influential business schools like Harvard and Stanford that were the first to introduce learning of strategic design management practices. The design approach they suggested was flexible and it allowed managers to be flexible and iterative wherein they could analyze new situations by constantly engaging with stakeholders and adapting projects.

Today strategic design thinking is being deployed as a problem-solving tool across a wide range of areas. Strategists use it to identify and visualize needs from complex and dynamic situations. In the next section, we discuss the Cobra Effect, a classic case study on the failure of strategic design thinking.

The Cobra Effect

While there are countless examples of a failure of strategy due to oversight, the story of the cobra effect is perhaps the most fascinating. Coined by the German economist Horst Siebert, the 'Cobra Effect' is one phenomenon that has continued to amuse strategic planners for a long time. This phenomenon refers to a situation where a simplistic attempted solution to a problem could make the problem even worse.

The story dates back to the old colonial days in Delhi, India. The British government discovered that the population of cobras in the city was on the rise. People were dying of snake bites, which scared many from stepping out of their houses. Worried that the situation could become hazardous, the government announced that anyone bringing a dead cobra would win a silver coin from the government.

The results of this decision were quite impressive, as residents began killing a large number of cobras. However, it was observed that after a short-term dip, the population of cobras started rising again. This sudden rise was because people had started breeding cobras to earn silver coins from the government.

When the news of this new development reached the government, it scrapped the reward programme. The cobra breeders were now holding worthless snakes that would provide no returns. Annoyed by the government's sudden decision they set the worthless snakes free. This resulted in a sudden increase in the population of wild cobras and the result was a situation that was even worse than the original problem.

The Rat Hunt in Hanoi

In 1995, while working for his doctoral project in Hanoi, Vietnam, which was once under French colonial rule, Michael G. Vann came across a bizarre story. Vann came across a folder labelled 'Destruction of Hazardous Animals: Rats', which detailed the number of rats killed every day and the payout to rat hunters.

Paul Doumer arrived in Hanoi as the newly appointed Governor-General of Indochina in 1897. Hanoi was poised to be transformed under him and he began working on Hanoi's infrastructure. Of the many things Doumer did was to build over 19 km of sewers. A large portion of the sewers lay beneath the French Quarter.

However, the new sewer system resulted in the rise of rats. Although rats were always present in Hanoi, the sewer system offered them a perfect habitat. Food was plenty and there were no predators. This, combined with the fact that a pair of rats could produce an average of seven litters a year, led to an explosion in rodent population.

When the population of rodents exploded, the frequency

of rats visiting the French Quarter around 1902 increased drastically, making the officials of the Indochina government panicky. Matters worsened when reports of a bubonic plague outbreak in the French Quarter began to emerge.

The government promptly responded by hiring and dispatching Vietnamese rat catching teams who began working inside the sewer system. The idea was to kill the rats. Each hunter was to be rewarded in proportion to the number of rodents they eliminated.

The hunters worked hard in the dark cramped sewer system and proved their worth. In the first week of the programme the hunters killed about 8,000 rats. The numbers rose to over 4,000 per day till it touched more than 20,000 on 12 June. However, it was observed that despite such efforts there was no noticeable change in the rodent population. Desperation drove the government to add vigilantes to the team of hunters and a one cent bounty was placed upon each rat. Anyone could claim the reward by presenting a rat tail to the authorities.

Within days there was a flood of Vietnamese handing rat tails to government officials. However, the city saw the appearance of tail-less rats. Upon investigation it was discovered that the Vietnamese were cutting off the tails of rats and releasing then in the sewer system to breed more rats. Even more alarming was the discovery that entrepreneurial Vietnamese had set up some rat breeding operations on the outskirts of the city to claim the bounty. Frustrated, the government scrapped the bounty, which now made the rodents worth nothing. The breeders responded by releasing the captive rats, which in turn caused the rodent population to spiral. The situation was such that the rat population now was more than what it had been at the start.

This too was another example of the cobra effect. We encounter many such instances in the field of warfare, politics and business where the strategy has failed to offer the intended benefits. Such failures can be attributed to the inability of strategists to see the big picture, to undertake a very nuanced approach to problem solving.

No matter how interesting the strategy, it is advisable for strategists to think about how people would respond to the new idea that sounds great on paper. There is always a group of people who have a tendency to game the system and therefore it is important that strategies are tried, tested and well-thought before they are rolled out.

This is the challenge that strategists are struggling to face every day, despite their best efforts in strategic design. Such problems crop up when decision makers fail to take a 360 degree view of all possible outcomes before they implement a plan. Such strategic failings are plenty in number and can be seen in organizations across the world.

Handling Design Failure

Rita Gunther McGrath, a professor at Columbia Business School, has proposed a scheme to put intelligent failure to work. In her *Harvard Business Review* article titled 'Failing by Design,' (2011) she points that we can plan, manage, and learn from failures by following seven principles. These principles, she argues, can help organizations learn from failure.

Principle 1: Decide what success and failure would look like before you launch an initiative

In an organization, it was observed that different teams had different understandings of a product's selling point, which created a gap of understanding. This gap was identified well ahead of time and teams were put in sync to prevent a failure in the marketplace. Such timely intervention before reaching out to the market is a good strategy to counter failure.

Principle 2: Convert assumptions into knowledge

In handling an uncertain task it is important to address the individual bias of team members before commitments are made. In making an assumption it is natural for individuals to gravitate towards information that confirms what they already believe in. This is known as 'confirmation bias' which can lead to fundamental problems. Therefore to handle this issue it is important the team members record their assumptions well in advance and get these resolved by sharing these with team members. In organizations that do not record these assumptions, problems emerge when the assumptions in people's mind get converted into facts and lead to unsettled organizations and employees. This also prevents organizations from learning to manage information sensitively.

Principle 3: Be quick about it—fail fast

Failing early helps organizations in multiple ways. It helps to save additional resources and establishes the cause and effect early on. An effective way to ensure that failure happens early is to test the elements of the project towards the beginning. Agile Software Development is one such early failure approach that helps to produce robust software programmes by containing the elements that are likely to fail at a later stage.

Principle 4: Contain the downside risk—fail cheaply

Failing without incurring substantial costs is an interesting design strategy. Test a small-scale prototype before making a significant investment is always a better option, as it helps to contain financial losses. An example of this can be gathered from the Japanese cosmetics firm Kao and its willingness to manufacture floppy disks. Unsure of whether Kao floppy disks would sell, the company bought disks from another manufacturer and put the Kao label on them before offering them to customers. The market response was very positive and the company moved ahead with its product diversification plan. Had the response been negative, Kao could have stopped the project and saved substantial costs.

Principle 5: Limit the uncertainty

It makes sense for companies to cut down on the uncertainty when they want to venture into a new area. Venturing into areas in which organizations have lesser knowledge and that have contexts that are different from the organization's existing business context is not a good idea. When organizations minimize the number of uncertainties they reduce the risk. A good way to venture into a new area is to break a long-term project into smaller pieces that can be managed well.

Principle 6: Build a culture that celebrates intelligent failure

Organizations can benefit when they build a culture that encourages intelligent risk taking and doesn't punish people who fail. This ability to tolerate failure should be embraced as a culture in an organization. Having such a culture would mean that employees would be part of incremental innovation by trying out new initiatives without the fear of being ridiculed.

Principle 7: Codify and share what you learn

Capturing and transferring learning are great learning avenues for organizations. Learning from routine everyday tasks provides immense value to organizations and individuals. Having micro-learning opportunities is an effective way to ensure the transfer of knowledge across the organization. This implies a sense of competitiveness likely to set the organization miles ahead of its competitors.

6
USING GAME THEORY TO FORMULATE STRATEGIES

Modern master strategists usually have to deploy a wide range of tools and techniques to be able to make a decision. Over the course of the past century, we have witnessed the emergence of a rich compendium of scientific knowledge that has changed the ways in which we look at strategy. Game Theory is one such outstanding concept that has emerged to help us make robust strategic decisions.

Game theory is a method of studying strategic situations. As a sub-field of economics, game theory has been widely used across diverse fields of human endeavour, such as management, medical sciences, business, technology, sociology, and media. Game theory helps us understand how players might interact under various circumstances. Strategists use it to tackle difficult and unprecedented situations where they are able to select the most promising options from a wide range of outcomes.

In game theory, business is a game. Every move in a game sparks off moves by others. Game theory matters to businesses because we live in an interactive world where no economic agent can act or live independently. In all business interactions it is important that we anticipate results, negotiate deals, and identify the likes and dislikes of our trading partners and competitors. This in turn helps us to position ourselves accordingly, and also be prepared for future market conditions.

Game theory was originally developed by mathematician John von Neumann and Economist Oskar Morgenstern in the seminal work, *Theory of Games and Economic Behaviour*, in 1944. For them strategy was a complete plan which specified what choices the player will make in every possible solution.

For Neumann and Morgenstern, there are principally two types of games. The first is rule-based, where players interact according to specified rules of engagement. The second type consists of freewheeling games where players interact without external constraints. Business, they opine, is a complex mix of both types. So while the rule-based games are guided by Newton's third law of motion, which says that to every action there is a reaction, freewheeling games are guided by a principle which states that you cannot take away more than you bring to the game.

Today game theory has emerged as a revolution, particularly in the way it has helped improve business thinking. The result is evident in the way companies are no longer working in isolation, but are instead collaborating as business networks. Businesses now interact with one another in a sustained fashion where information is readily shared between them. Game theory enables us to examine these interactive and complex relationships to generate interesting win-win business strategies.

Conventional economics without game theory isn't of much help, as the assumptions are lopsided and it ignores the realm of intermediate interactions where most business activity takes place. Game theory tackles these interactions head-on.

Game theory has two main branches—non-cooperative game theory and cooperative game theory. Each of these branches is different from the other, as each has different uses. The two concepts are so different that the problems in one area cannot be solved by concepts borrowed from the other.

Non-Cooperative Game Theory

The most widely discussed branch of game theory is non-cooperative theory. It deals with situations where we interact with small numbers of other players whose strategic choices directly affect our payoffs and situations. Non-cooperative games provide insight on what payoffs individual players will receive, depending on their strategy and the strategies of other players.

Dr Nash's primary contribution to game theory was his ability to predict a balanced outcome of these games. He demonstrated that non-cooperative games result in what is called the 'Nash equilibrium.' Here, each player makes the optimal choice depending on what the other players might choose, even though these choices don't result in the best outcomes for everyone.

The Prisoner's Dilemma

The Prisoner's Dilemma is one of the best known examples of a non-cooperative game. It is also the most widely examined game in game theory that displays why two rational individuals might not cooperate even when doing so appears to be in their best interests. Originally ideated by Merrill Flood and Melvin Dresher in 1950, it was formalized with the prison sentence rewards outlined by Albert W. Tucker who named it the 'prisoner's dilemma.'

In this two members of a criminal gang are arrested and placed in two separate rooms for interrogation. Both these prisoners are given a set of rules and their outcomes, which are as follows:

- If one (Prisoner A) testifies against the other prisoner (Prisoner B) but Prisoner B does not testify against Prisoner A, then Prisoner A is set free and Prisoner B will get 3 years in jail (and vice versa).
- If both prisoners A and B testify against one another they will both be sentenced to two years in jail.
- If neither Prisoner A nor Prisoner B testifies against one another then each gets one year. The payout in this case is the highest as each receives a shorter jail sentence.

Here, confession is the dominant strategy as it offers each player the best payoff for each of the choices by the other player. Dominant strategies are strategies that are best regardless of what strategy the other player chooses. The double confession is the Nash equilibrium as none of the players can improve their payoff by adopting a different strategy. The Nash equilibrium was proposed by the mathematician and game theorist John Nash.

Simply defined, the Nash equilibrium can be understood as a set of best-response strategies deployed in a two-player game. The Nash equilibrium is an outcome where the strategy of player A is the best response to player B's strategy and player B's strategy is the best response to player A's strategy.

The prisoner's dilemma earns its popularity from its successful use in diverse settings. Till date it has been used across diverse fields such as environmental science, deciphering animal behaviour, psychology, economics, sports and international politics.

Applying the Prisoner's Dilemma in a Repeated Game

The prisoner's dilemma can also be applied equally well in a repeated game. A very good example of the Prisoner's Dilemma in a repeated game can be seen in the functioning of the Oil and Petroleum Exporting Countries (OPEC) and the game to control oil prices. Whenever the OPEC meets, member countries have to decide between either cheating (betraying) or colluding (cooperating) with others by deciding on the quantity of oil they would produce.

For OPEC to be considered a prisoner's dilemma the group must be better off as a collective than they would be as individual entities. To understand this let us look at the example of Saudi Arabia. Saudi Arabia could make a lot of additional money if they betrayed the collective and produced and sold more oil than what they agreed to. In such a situation, Saudi Arabia would get a larger share of the global market. But when they do so, the group would be at the receiving end since the price of oil will come down and so would the revenues. Now, if Saudi Arabia cooperated with other competing countries of OPEC and did not increase production the price of crude would increase and benefit everyone in the group. The result of this would be higher profits for everyone in the group.

Similar experiences are also visible in other business environments. Every time a business spends on expensive promotions to match a competitor's price promotion, both the businesses will lose revenues that pass on the benefits to customers. This may not be so if no businesses spend on promotions.

Applying the Prisoner's Game with n-Persons

The n-person prisoner's dilemma (NPD) is when it is applied where there are more than two players. NPD emerged in the 1970s and ever since it has been used to model several real-world problems. One of these real-world problems was the theory of the 'invisible hand' proposed by economist Adam Smith in 1976.

Use of the NPD in the labour market is best described in the following situation. All trade unions try to negotiate wages so that these wages exceed the rate of inflation in the economy. But when all trade unions negotiate wages to benefit their own interests, the prices of goods and services go up, leaving everyone worse off. In order to resolve this, the British Labour Party issued a manifesto in 1974 that intended to convince trade unions to exercise restraint. The party wanted these trade unions to be part of the 'social contract' so as to ensure collective rationality over individual rationality.

The Tragedy of Commons

Another interesting example of a NPD is the tragedy of commons. To understand this we have to consider the case of six farmers each with a cow that weighs 1000 lbs. All these six farmers share a plot of grazing land that can sustain a maximum of only 6 cows. If any additional cow is introduced then the weight of the existing cows will decrease by 100 lbs.

We assume that each farmer gets the opportunity to add one cow. In that case, when one farmer adds another cow he gets two cows weighing 900 lbs each. If each of these farmers acts only on their self-interest, then each farmer is left with two cows that weigh 400 lbs each instead of one cow with a weight of 1000 lbs. This was the NPD situation that impoverished small farmers in England in the eighteenth century.

Thus all multi-person prisoner's dilemmas have a structure where any game satisfying a set of criteria gets qualified as an NPD. The first criterion suggests that every player has two options (cooperate or defect). The second criterion points out that defecting remains the dominant strategy as each player appears to be better off by choosing to defect than to cooperate. The third criterion suggests that the dominant strategies (to defect) intersect at a point of equilibrium even though the outcome is worse when all players choose to defect.

The Cooperative Game Theory

The Cooperative Game Theory is a branch of game theory that has even more diverse applications in business. The cooperative game theory earns its name from its ability to deal with situations in which players make cooperative agreements to carry out joint strategies and share the payoffs. Business people usually deploy the cooperative game theory whenever they set up a new business or a new combination of businesses.

In the cooperative type of engagement players do not focus on specific moves or strategies; rather, they look at the way players interact and arrange themselves into groups with the sole objective of creating different amounts of value. Cooperative game theory is especially useful when businesses decide the people and assets to include in a business, constituents of a corporation and the corporations to be included in an alliance. It also helps determine the exact value that individual units can expect to gather in exchange for their participation. For example, it can be a powerful tool for assessing several things such as the viability of new ventures, products, technologies, distribution and supply channels and markets.

Unlike the non-cooperative game theory, cooperative game theory focuses on groupings. Instead of payoffs, cooperative game theory talks of the value that would be created by the possible combination of players. The cooperative game theory seeks to identify the groupings that are likely to be more stable as the players will not be able to do better by defecting to another group.

When deciding how the participants are to divide the payouts in a cooperative game we use the solution provided by the Shapley Value. Lloyd Shapley provided this solution in the year 1953. While arriving at the Shapley Value requires us to deploy a mathematical calculation, it is essential to understand that the Shapley Value is one way to distribute the total gains to the players, assuming that all players collaborate. The Shapley Value was enhanced and developed for situations such as infinite games.

For the master strategist, deploying the cooperative game theory would provide them ways to decide about payoffs to participants when a large number of players collaborate. For instance, in a situation where there is a large team, the strategist may use the cooperative strategy to decide how to reward different team members so as to ensure that none are left disenchanted. Without the cooperative game theory it is difficult to satisfy individual team members, who may turn hostile and destroy the team's collective value.

The GM Card Programme—Applying the Game Theory

An interesting application of the game theory can be seen in the way a lose-lose scheme was changed to a win-win situation, as described by Brandenburger and Nalebaff (1995). In September 1992, General Motor and Household Bank issued a new credit card system that allowed 5 per cent off of their charges for buying or leasing a new GM car. The limit for this was about $500 per year and a maximum of $3,500. The card was so popular that within a month it had 1.2 million subscribers and in two years the number touched 8.7 million.

The card helped draw Ford car buyers towards GM (a win-lose strategy). But after launching the card, GM removed all previous incentives that it offered to car buyers. When this discount was reduced, non-card holders ended up paying the price of a GM car for a Ford car. The programme therefore allowed Ford to raise its prices, which in turn, also allowed GM to raise its prices without the fear of losing customers to Ford. The result was a win-win situation between GM and Ford.

The impact of the aforementioned GM card programme can be best deciphered only through the game theory. The subtle aspects of the programme must be seen from an allocentric perspective i.e. understand how competitors of GM such as Ford, Volkswagen and others respond to GM's card programme.

Evidently, the mindset of seeing business as war is a flawed strategy. Sometimes the best way to succeed is to let others do well. When the situation is win-win, others offer less resistance making it easier for the business to succeed.

7
MODERN THEORIES OF ORGANIZATIONAL STRATEGY

Modern strategists operate in a complex terrain. In order to function optimally they may need to derive essential knowledge, not only from the wisdom of the past, but also from the wisdom that emerged in the twentieth and twenty-first centuries. It was this era that saw the formulation of many interesting theories on strategy that were conceptualized and implemented in the corporate world.

In this chapter we explore some of these essential theories that impinge on organizational strategy in diverse ways, both intrinsically or extrinsically.

Porter's Five Forces Analysis

Porter's Five Forces is a framework or model to identify and analyze five competitive forces that shape every industry. This framework, originally developed by Professor Michael E. Porter of Harvard University in 1979, helps us determine the industry's weaknesses and strengths. This model is frequently deployed to help identify an industry's structure so as to determine its corporate strategy.

Porter's model (Fig. 7.1) is extremely flexible and can be applied to any segment of the economy to search for profitability and attractiveness. The Five Forces model looks at five specific factors that determine whether a business can be profitable or not. Porter developed his Five Forces analysis in reaction to the then—popular SWOT analysis.

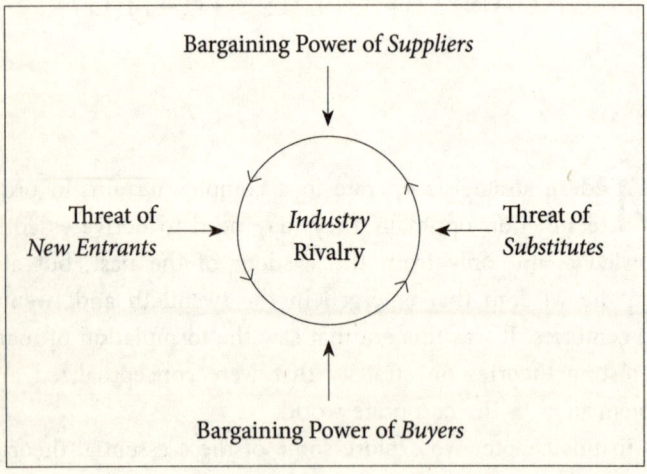

Fig. 7.1: Porter's Five Forces Model

[Although the original diagram provided by Porter in his paper in the *Harvard Business Review* had a slightly different title, the essence remains the same.]

The five basic forces are as follows:

1. **Threat of new entrants**: The seriousness of the threat posed by new entrants depends on the barriers and the reaction from existing competitors. If barriers to entry are high the entrants can expect sharp retaliation from competitors.

There are six major barriers to entry that include:
a. Economies of scale
    Here economies deter entry by forcing the entrant to enter on a large scale or accept a cost disadvantage.
b. Product differentiation
    Brand identification serves as a barrier and forces entrants to spend heavily to overcome customer loyalty.
c. Capital requirements
    This refers to the large capital expenditure that new entrants have to make in order to be able to compete
d. Cost disadvantages independent of size.
    Here incumbents can have advantage over new entrants in terms of proprietary technology, preferential access to raw materials, favourable geographical locations, established brand identities or cumulative experience.
e. Access to distribution channels
    Here new entrants struggle to find access to distribution channels such as the space in the supermarket shelves that must be replaced by price breaks, promotions, etc.
f. Government policy
    The government can limit or even foreclose the entry off new companies by deploying such things as license requirements and limits imposed on access to raw materials. The government can also affect the entry barriers by deploying controls related to pollution, etc.

2. **Threat of substitute products or services**
   Substitutes perform the same function as the industry's products or services but they do it differently. For example, videoconferencing is a substitute for travel and plastic is a substitute for aluminum. Substitutes are always present but they may be disguised in some other form. They limit the profits and also reduce the bonanza that companies can

expect when the industry is booming.
3. **Bargaining power of customers (Buyers)**
   Powerful customers can impact the industry by forcing down the prices, demanding better quality or more services. They can do this at the cost of industry profitability. However, the bargaining power can vary across customers depending on the volume in which they buy.
4. **Bargaining power of suppliers**
   Suppliers have the ability to exert bargaining power on buyers by increasing the price of raw materials. Supplier groups can be powerful depending on the uniqueness of the product, which makes them ask for higher prices.
5. **Industry rivalry**
   Rivalry among competitors can be seen in the familiar forms of jockeying such as price competition, introduction of products and slugfests through advertisements which can hurt the bottom-line. The intensity of rivalry, in turn, is dependent on many other factors such as number of competitors, pace of industry growth, fixed costs, exit barriers etc.

Mintzberg's 5Ps of Strategy

In 1987, a Canadian management expert, Henry Mintzberg, developed the 5Ps of Strategy. These 5Ps can be used by an organization to develop a more robust and effective strategy. Each of these five areas helps us to approach strategy from a different perspective that can take complete advantage of an organization's strengths and capabilities.

Mintzberg proposed the 5Ps to help understand strategy more effectively. This not only helps to handle strategy but also compels us to think through a variety of different angles that we would ordinarily not consider. The five perspectives are as follows:

- Strategy has a Plan
- Strategy has a Ploy
- Strategy has a Pattern
- Strategy has a Position
- Strategy has a Perspective

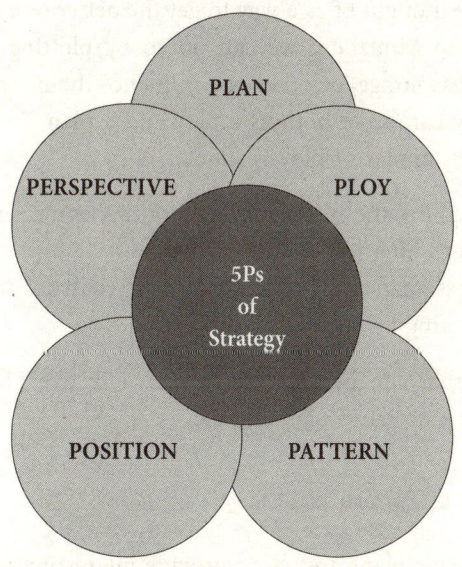

Fig. 7.2: Mintzberg's 5Ps of Strategy

1. Strategy as a Plan

Any good strategy must have a plan. A plan is a course of action or a set of guidelines that strategists want to follow. Plans can be developed by brainstorming the various options and then deciding on the ones we want to include. Plans are usually developed in advance.

Planning is required when people think of strategy development. There are various tools of planning which include PEST analysis, SWOT analysis, etc.

2. Strategy as Ploy

Ploy can be thought of as a way to get the better of a competitor. According to Mintzberg we can do so by plotting to disrupt, dissuade, discourage, or otherwise influence them. This is where the strategy can serve both as a ploy and a plan.

Some examples of ploys include:

- Dropping the price of cars to outwit competitors
- Threatening legal action
- Investing in cutting-edge areas like Analytics and Machine Learning

The tools that can be used to develop effective ploys include game theory, scenario planning etc.

3. Strategy as Pattern

While strategic plans and ploys provide interesting information, they do not provide an understanding of how a behaviour from the past and present has impacted and continues to impact the organization.

So while the plan can be perceived as the intended strategy, the pattern can be seen as the realized strategy. In looking at strategy as a pattern we try to understand what patterns have worked for us. Try to gather information about the impact of the pattern for frontline teams and the support staff. The pattern will give you a good idea on how to approach strategic planning. Patterns can be determined by deploying the 'Core Competency Model'.

To understand how an organization can deploy strategy as a pattern, let us consider a multi-national company that decides to enter the Indian market by making business decisions based on the particular needs of Indian customers. If the pattern yields great results the MNC may want to continue with that. If the MNC realizes partial success it will have to take another look at this pattern and think of deploying a more contextual product strategy that is attuned to the needs of the Indian market.

4. Strategy as Position

Another way to define the strategy is to list it on the basis of the 'position.' This position helps you to determine where you stand with respect to competition. By defining strategy in terms of the position we can find a fit between the organization and the environment in which it operates, between the internal and the external world. This in turn helps to develop a sustainable competitive advantage.

There could be many ways in which you can position your company. You can either develop a niche product to position yourself ahead of competition or you may decide to be one of several players in the market.

5. Strategy as Perspective

Perspective helps to shape up the personality and culture of the organization. Every business goes to the market with its own unique perspective. Some organizations go to the market with a focus on quality and cost control while others want to be seen as innovative.

The perspective strategy should meet the organization's culture. For instance, if the organization wants to be quality conscious then its culture should reflect that in letter and spirit. A quality conscious hospital should have neat and organized infrastructure.

Core Competence

Complexity theory is an interdisciplinary field that was introduced in 1990 by C.K. Prahalad and Gary Hamel. To understand the idea of core competency metaphorically, Prahalad and Hamel provide this story (Fig. 7.3):

> The diversified corporation is a large tree. The trunk and major limbs are core products, the smaller branches are business units; the leaves, flowers, and fruit are end products. The root system that provides nourishment, sustenance, and stability is the core competence. (*Harvard Business Review*, May-June 1990)

In ideating core competence, Prahalad and Hamel present a certain broad canvas of core competence:

- Core competencies are collective learnings in the organization
- Core competency is the delivering of value
- Core competency is communication, involvement and a deep commitment to work across organizational boundaries
- Core competencies do not diminish with use; rather they are enhanced as they are applied and shared
- Global leadership is waged on three different planes—core competence, core products, and end products

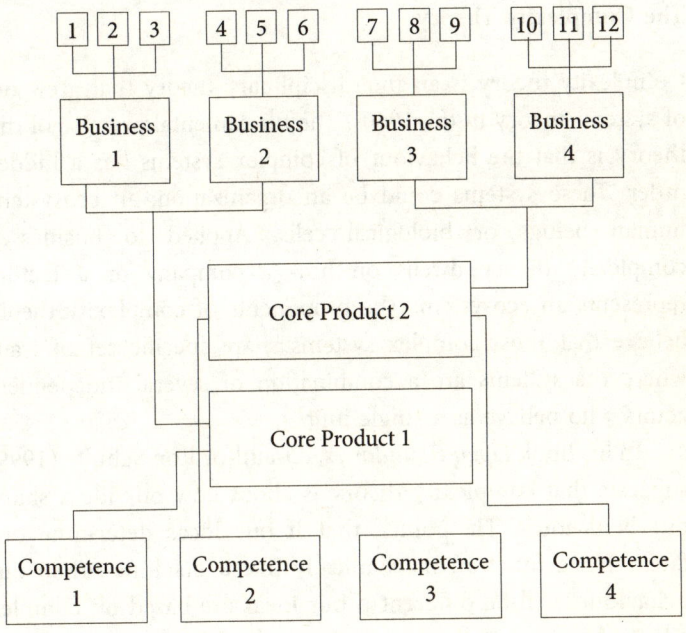

Fig. 7.3: Core Products are nourished by Core Competencies that function as the root

Three tests can be applied to identify the core competencies in an organization.

They outlined three tests that can be applied to determine whether something is a core competence or not.

First, a core competency provides access to a wide variety of markets. For instance a competency in semiconductor chips allows a company to be part of diverse businesses as desktops, laptops, tabs, mobiles, IoT devices etc. Second, a core competency should significantly contribute to the perceived customer benefits of the end product. Third, a core competency should be difficult for competitors to imitate.

The Complexity Theory

Complexity theory is an interdisciplinary theory that grew out of systems theory in the 1960s. The fundamental premise of this theory is that the behaviour of complex systems has a hidden order. These systems could be an organization, an ecosystem, human beings or biological cells. Applied to businesses, complexity theory dwells on how a company or a factory represents an ecosystem. The proponents of complexity theory believe that most complex systems share specific set of traits where the systems are a combination of several independent actors who behave as a single unit.

In his book *Open Boundaries*, co-author Ron Schultz (1999) suggests that complexity theory is about how our ideas shape our behaviours. He points, that if our ideas determine our fates—if we function mechanically like a machine—then our behaviours will be different if our ideas are based on complex adaptive systems that are evolutionary and organic. Complexity theory helps organizations to thrive in an environment of ambiguity and unpredictability that are the characteristics of modern businesses.

Scholars feel that the organization of a system is not accidental but the result of laws of nature that we do not completely understand. An important concept of the complexity theory is that the actors in the system interact with one another and undergo spontaneous self-organization without anyone being in charge of the system. It is believed that this happens because the agents/actors are constantly adapting to one another.

In the absence of a master controller of any system we experience coherent system behaviour generated by the competition and cooperation between actors. In the book *Complexity: A Very Short Introduction* John Holland (2014) points out that as they gain experience, complex adaptive systems constantly revise and rearrange their building blocks. He explains this phenomenon by suggesting that a firm may promote individuals who do well and also reshuffle itself for achieving greater efficiency.

Another interesting aspect of the complexity theory is the assumption that there are principles underlying all emergent properties. These principles emerge from the interactions of different actors. An analogy of this is forwarded by David Berreby who suggests that no individual ant makes the decision on when an ant colony should switch to a better food source. This decision is a result of the ants' interactions.

Businesses use complexity theory to encourage innovative thinking and real-time responses to change by allowing business units to self-organize. However for the complexity theory to work effectively, organizational leaders have to let go of rigid controls of these systems. Organizations stand to gain more by stepping back from routine tasks and watching for emergent properties and patterns. Those conditions or patterns have the ability to bring effective solutions for a progressive future.

However, complexity theory should not be seen as a panacea for all organizations. The ideas of complexity theory emanate from the assumption that employees in these companies are intelligent, enthusiastic, and willing to work in teams with very little management intervention. In reality the situation may be the opposite and employees may require more intervention of the management to function properly.

Dynamic Capabilities Framework

This framework, forwarded by Teece et. al. (1997) in their paper 'Dynamic Capabilities and Strategic Management,' refers to the capability of an organization to deal with combined internal and external resources as well as the capabilities of doing business in environments of rapid technological change. The initial definition put forward by Teece et. al. (1997) puts Dynamic Capabilities (DC) as 'the firm's ability to integrate, build, and reconfigure internal and external competences to address rapidly changing environments.'

However, over the years, DC has undergone several changes in the way it is defined. Some viewed DC as tools to gain competitive advantage while others posited it as a learning process that is in accordance with something that an organization undertakes. These opinions and counter-opinions have not only muddled the waters but have kept the exact meaning of Dynamic Capabilities quite confusing. However, for the sake of convenience many still follow Teece et. al.'s work as a guiding force.

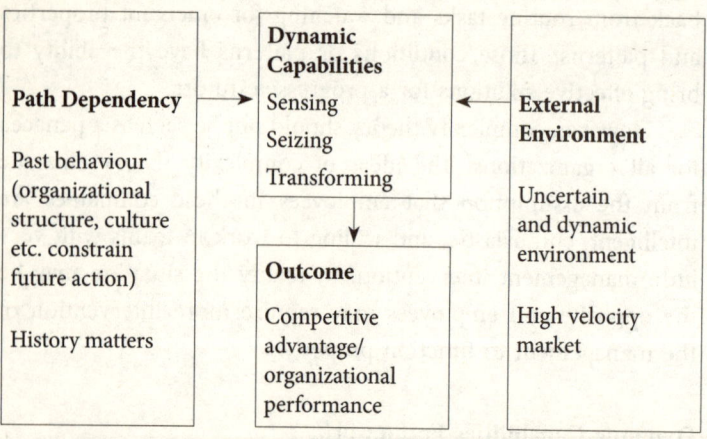

Fig. 7.4: The dynamic capabilities framework (based on Teece et. al., 1997)

Thus, DC can be defined in terms of the actions taken to adjust a company's resources into innovative forms of competitive advantage. The fundamental assumption of this framework is that the core competencies should be used to modify short-term competitive positions which in turn help build a longer-term competitive advantage.

This framework does not prescribe anything but serves as an interpretative tool that helps to examine the relationships between capabilities and organizational performance in a dynamic setting. The framework emphasizes the following:

Path dependency—This suggests that in order to understand how the resource base of an organization can be used to address change, we must examine how past actions have influenced the current trajectory. When we do so we will get a good idea of how the future will be affected by current actions.

Three types of adjustments—The framework defines three types of activities and adjustments that can be undertaken. These three types are:

i. **Sensing**—Refers to activities such as scanning, learning and interpretation through which an opportunity can be identified and assessed.
ii. **Seizing**—Refers to the use of activities through which a sensed opportunity can be utilized.
iii. **Transforming**—Refers to the process of resource configuration through which the organization is continuously renewed.

However, despite its potential, Teece agreed that the dynamic capabilities theory is not tightly predictive. He opined that it is difficult for organizations to figure out the most important capabilities. Nevertheless, Teece thinks that the dynamic capabilities theory provides an intellectual structure for businesses to start thinking about why companies succeed or fail.

PEST & PESTLE

The PEST analysis framework is extremely useful in strategic planning. It helps us to understand the various macro-environmental influences on business. These influences may include political, economic, social and technological forces often used in the environmental scope of this process. In order to remove the negative connotation of the PEST acronym, many have reworked it as STEP.

Table 7.1: Example of a PEST analysis

POLITICAL	ECONOMIC
• Environmental issues	• Home economy trends
• Current legislation	• Regional economy trends
• Future legislation	• Global economy trends
• International legislation	• General taxation issues
• Current regulatory issues	• Market and trade cycles
• Government policies	• Industry factors
• Funding and grants	• Buying power of consumers
• Lobbying and pressure groups	• Employment trends
SOCIAL	**TECHNOLOGICAL**
• Lifestyle trends	• Technological trends
• Demographics	• Development of competing technologies
• Consumer attitudes and opinions	• Research funding
• Brand and company image	• Information and communications
• Consumer buying patterns	• Innovation potential
• Major events and influences	• Intellectual property issues
• Attitude towards products & services	• Global communications

The results obtained from a PEST analysis are often used either to take advantage of potential opportunities or to make contingency plans when preparing business or strategic plans. Table 7.1 provides a broad idea of the way we do PEST analysis. At times, PEST may also include two more areas—legal and environmental—that transforms PEST into 'PESTLE'.

The scope of PEST analysis is virtually limitless, and therefore for the PEST analysis to succeed, it is important to define its scope so that contributors remain focused. Defining the scope also helps the ones who interpret the results.

Ideally, once you acquire knowledge about your current market, you can deploy a SWOT analysis. A PEST (or PESTLE) analysis looks at the market, SWOT analysis looks at your business. In this sense a SWOT analysis helps you gather holistic data.

Scenario Planning

Scenario planning, also called 'Scenario and Contingency Planning' is a structured mechanism that organisations use to evaluate the future. The process involves having a group of executives who develop a handful of scenarios for the company. These stories relate to what developments the future might unfold and in turn affect other issues. These issues could be narrow, such as, what geographical region to make the next investment in, whether the company should go online with a portal etc. Issues could be even broader: a German authority, for instance, contemplating the impact of changing demography on new schools.

Some of the world's popular organizations like Motorola, Disney and Accenture have been using scenario planning to seek answers about the future. In the 1970s, scenario planning was very popular due to primarily two reasons. The first relates to the dissatisfaction with existing ways of planning that had given misleading results. The second relates to the idea that businesses can benefit from the non-rational side of human nature.

In his *Harvard Business Review* article, 'Scenarios: Unchartered Waters Ahead', Pierre Wack (1985) offered a very interesting explanation of scenarios. He pointed that scenarios primarily deal with two distinct worlds—one of 'facts' and the other of 'perceptions'. So even when these scenarios appear to search for facts, in reality, they look for perceptions inside the heads of decision-makers. Their objective is to collect and transform information of strategic significance into fresh perceptions.

Participants begin scenario planning with a long discussion on how big shifts in society—economics, politics and technology—might affect a particular issue. Following this the group draws up a list of priorities such as the things that will have the maximum impact on the issue being discussed and whose outcome is the most uncertain. This process helps sketch out rough pictures of the future.

Scenario planning borrows from wider disciplines and interests such as economics, psychology, politics and demographics. Such consolidation of knowledge suggests, amongst other things, the presence of a creative side to the scenario planning strategy.

In the everyday, scenario planning is something that humans undertake all the time. In their book, *Scenario Planning: The Link Between Future and Strategy*, Lindgren and Bandhold articulate the role of scenario planning quite effectively. They suggest that the healthy human brain is 'constantly writing scenarios, interpreting signals in the environment and reframing them into meaningful images of and trajectories into the future.'

Without being able to draw scenarios humans would not

have been able to derive alternate strategies. And without these alternate strategies, coping with the world we live in would have been extremely difficult.

The essence of it is summed up perfectly by Michael Porter: 'The essence of strategy is choosing what not to do.'

8

CONCLUSION

To think of strategy is to think of a complex mesh of concepts, activities, and techniques that can be fused together to develop a roadmap for progress. Today we witness a dramatic shift in the form and character of master strategists—the leaders who lead the transformation and growth. Modern strategists are new-age reincarnations of the older military-political leaders who have toiled to transform the fate of entire civilizations, nations, and regions. Today's master strategists represent a plethora of interests and affiliations spread across the socio-political and corporate-business space.

This changing role of modern-day strategists compels them to embrace an equally diverse set of activities to accomplish their goals. Their engagement is complex and far-fetched and they address a whole range of actors and stakeholders. This makes master strategists a critical part of leadership today.

We have also witnessed a shift in the traditional sense of power that master strategists enjoy. Earlier, the sense of power was more direct and derived from military victories and conquests. Today this sense of power has become more subtle, indirect, and area-specific.

We are also confronting a raging debate about the impossibility of having master strategists. In his book *Strategy:*

A History, Lawrence Freedman suggests that the master strategist requires a wide range of expertise and a holistic vision. Such professionals, he feels, are difficult to find. He further suggests that strategies are rarely developed by professional strategists and are a result of leaders who try to impose their will. These leaders, Freedman believes, cannot grasp all the effects of their actions; nor are they able to understand the dynamic complexity of the system of which they are a part. So it is perhaps unwise to expect too much from strategists. Freedman also points to the exalted view of the 'strategic man' who does not appear in reality, by pointing to the distinct separation between the military and political spheres.

Daniel Steed argued that the state system is large and cumbersome and has several moving parts, which make managing it such a daunting task. But despite this, he feels that the strategic man cannot be a myth. He feels that the separation of the military sphere from the political has created 'difficult conditions' for the strategic man to emerge. For Steed, the strategic man is not the 'Supreme Being,' but someone who is good enough, such as President Eisenhower, President Ronald Reagan, US army General David Petraeus (who led forces in Iraq), and countless others from contemporary history who provide hope.

In certain quarters there is also a belief that the breed of natural or instinctive strategists is on a decline and has been replaced by a more rational, number-driven, mechanical form. Many companies also remain oriented towards incremental improvement-bettering performance in areas they are already engaged in. This mechanization of strategic planning appears to have made critical thinking obsolete.

However, there are good reasons why the real master strategist can never emerge from such structured environments and initiatives. And the reason for this is simple. If all strategists try to follow the beaten path and deploy the same tools, techniques and technologies, the resultant output would all be the same. This means that the strategic advantage that organizations yearn to realize will cease to exist. When such differences vanish the strategic advantage vanishes too.

Therefore, in becoming a master strategist one has to tread a strange territory. On the one hand, they should be aware of all the advancement in diverse strategic knowledge that has taken place over more than a century. But in their application of strategy they have to devise their own style and form. There are no rules when the master strategists apply strategy.

The traditional idea of strategy has paved the way to newer forms like the grand strategy. The twenty-first century master strategists have adapted to these new formulations and in doing so they have embraced new concepts and themes that are contextual and relevant.

Mastering strategic thinking is the key to becoming a skilled strategist. In essence the objective of strategic thinking is not merely to develop powerful strategies by deploying a set of strategic thinking models; instead it seeks to promulgate the development of a strategic mindset. Since no two strategic situations can be exactly the same, it is pertinent that the master strategist focuses on developing a mindset that enables them to resolve strategic challenges irrespective of the difficulty. Even though working on strategies by drawing analogies with instances from the past appears helpful, it may not be always very helpful in dealing with situations that are new and unknown.

Over the years countless decision-making models have been floated for the strategist to be able to make a good decision. The challenge is to sift through these models and adopt the one that provides the most efficient strategic formulations. Selecting the model that best fits a particular situation is something that is left to the subjective interpretation of strategists themselves.

In organizations the components for strategic thought and action follow a certain pattern. Using a wide variety of tools the strategist can unveil intricate aspects of organizational strategy. Strategic purpose and strategic planning are two crucial aspects of this organizational strategy.

Any strategic formulation is guided by psychological theories that can impinge on the way we formulate strategy. At an operational level strategies in organizations are delineated into distinct categories such as corporate strategy, business strategy, functional strategy, and operating strategy. Other forms of classification of strategy have also been proposed. Deploying the organizational grand strategy also serves as a broad canvas of strategic intervention.

Modern day expertise of organizational strategy can be seen in the increasing demand for 'Decision Scientists,' who have come to occupy a centrality in organizational decision making at its highest levels.

Some of the most promising scope for developing robust strategies can be seen in Design Thinking and Game Theory. These tools or concepts are prescribed as the modern ways of mastering strategy formulation.

Design thinking represents a new perspective of managing strategy. It focuses on developing strategies where the emphasis is on 'thinking by doing,' which suggests the need to get into the thick of things rather than wasting time on planning. It is a more creative approach that is flexible and accommodative in a distinctive way. The application of design thinking offers a way to undertake 'Strategic Design Thinking' that provides actionable solutions. Global organizations have begun deploying strategic design thinking to formulate many features in their service and product portfolios. The crux here is to look at strategy as 'strategy+action'.

The next prescription for the master strategist would be to borrow from the advances in the fields of Game Theory. Game Theory offers a new way to visualize problem solving and decision making. Both the cooperative and non-cooperative theories of game theory can be applied to different situations in businesses to arrive at unique solutions. The game theory and its ever-expanding ocean of knowledge is the Holy Grail for master strategists.

Perhaps the most important lesson that strategists need to understand is that the insights and unique streams of knowledge that come through experience are difficult to gather. Experiences—from the mundane to the profound—remain the most significant bastion of strategies. Experiential learning also becomes significant because experiences are gathered through one's own observation and are simply non-replicable and unique.

We must also embrace values inspired by right thinking. In today's fast-changing conditions, survival depends on our mastery of the changing world. As writer and editor Alvin Toffler says, good strategy requires constant learning, unlearning, and relearning, and it calls for a shift from strategy as planning to strategy as learning.

BIBLIOGRAPHY

Ackoff, R. L. (1981). *Creating the Corporate Future*, New York: John Wiley & Sons.

Acks, A. (2018). *The Bubble of Confirmation Bias: Critical Thinking about Digital Media*. Enslow Publishing: New York.

Aguilar, O. (2003). 'How strategic performance management is helping companies create business value'. *Strategic Finance* (January): 44-49.

Alcacer, J. and M. Zhao. (2012). 'Local R&D strategies and multilocation firms: The role of internal linkages'. *Management Science* (April): 734-753.

Alkhafaji, A.F. (2003). *Strategic Management: Formulation, Implementation, and Control in a Dynamic Environment*. Haworth Press: New York.

Amram, M. (2002). *Value Sweep: Mapping Corporate Growth Opportunities*. Harvard Business School Press: Boston.

Andersen, T. J. (2004). 'Integrating Decentralized Strategy Making and Strategic Planning Processes in Dynamic Environments.' *Journal of Management Studies* 41, no. 8: 1271-99.

Anderson, C. R. and F. T. Paine. (1975). 'Managerial perceptions and strategic behaviour'. *The Academy of Management Journal* 18(4): 811-823.

Anderson, C. (2006). *The Long Tail*. New York: Hyperion.

Anderson, J. and C. Markides. (2007). 'Strategic innovation at the base of the pyramid'. *MIT Sloan Management Review* (Fall): 83-88.

Andrews, K. R. (1971). *The Concept of Corporate Strategy*. Dow-Jones Irwin.

Andrews, K. R. and D. K. D. (1987). *The Concept of Corporate Strategy*. Homewood, IL: R. D. Irwin, 1987.

Ansoff, H. I. (1969). *Business Strategy: Selected Readings*. New York: Penguin Books, 1969.

Ansoff, H. I. (1965). *Corporate Strategy: An Analytic Approach to Business Policy for Growth and Expansion*. New York: McGraw-Hill, 1965.

Ansoff, H. I. (1991). 'Critique of Henry Mintzberg's "The Design School: Reconsidering the Basic Premises of Strategic Management"'. *Strategic Management Journal* 12, no. 6 (1991): 449-61.

Balkcom, J. E., C. D. Ittner and D. F. Larcker. (1997). 'Strategic performance measurement: Lessons learned and future directions'. *Journal of Strategic Performance Measurement* 1(2): 22-32.

Banker, R. D., H. Chang and M. Pizzini. (2011). 'The judgmental effects of strategy maps in balanced scorecard performance evaluations'. *International Journal of Accounting Information Systems* 12(4): 259-279.

Barnes, D. (2008). *Operation Management: An International Perspective*. Thomson Learning. London.

Begley, T. M. and D. P. Boyd. (2003). 'The need for a corporate global mind-set'. *MIT Sloan Management Review* (Winter): 25-32.

Beiman, I. (2006). 'Using the balanced scorecard methodology to execute China strategy'. *Cost Management* (July/August): 9-19.

Ben-Hur, S., B. Jaworski and D. Gray. (2015). 'Aligning corporate learning with strategy'. *MIT Sloan Management Review* (Fall): 53-59.

Betz, F. (2016). *Strategic Thinking: A Comprehensive Guide*. Emerald Group Publishing: United Kingdom.

Birnbaum, M.H. and Birnbaum, M.O. (2000). *Psychological Experiments on the Internet*. California: Elsevier.

Bolman, L. G., and Deal, T. E., Reframing Organizations, Jossey-Bass, San Francisco, 1991.

Brands, H. (2012). *The Promise and Pitfalls of Grand Strategy*. U. S. Army War College.

Brunt, P. A., 'Spartan Policy and Strategy in the Archidamian War,' *Phoenix* 19 (1965) 255-280.

Campbell, S. (2015, October 1). 'The 10 Mental Skills Necessary to Become a Strategic Visionary'. Retrieved from https://www.entrepreneur.com/article/251224

Carr, C. and D. Collis. (2011). 'Should you have a global strategy?' *MIT Sloan Management Review* (Fall): 21-24.

Carr, C., K. Kolehmainen and F. Mitchell. (2010). 'Strategic investment decision making practices: A contextual approach'. *Management Accounting Research* (September): 167-184.

Chandler, A. D. (1962). *Strategy and Structure: Chapters in the History of the American Industrial Enterprise*. Cambridge, MA: MIT Press.

Cherry, K. (2019). 'The Psychology of Decision-Making Strategies'. Very Well Mind. Retrieved from https://www.verywellmind.com/decision-making-strategies-2795483

Cleary, T.F. (1992). The Japanese Art of War: Understanding the Culture of Strategy. Shambhala Publications: Colorado.

Clemons, E. K. and Santamaria J. A. (2002). Maneuver warfare: Can modern military strategy lead you to victory? *Harvard Business Review* (April): 56-65.

Collins, J. C. and J. I. P. (1996). Building your company's vision. *Harvard Business Review* (September-October): 65-77.

Daniels, J. L. and Daniels N. C. (1993). Global Vision: Building New Models for the Corporation of the Future, McGraw-Hill, New York, 1993.

Davenport, T. H. (2016). Rise of the strategy machines. *MIT Sloan Management Review* (Fall): 13-16.

David Hussey. (2001). 'Creative Strategic Thinking and the Analytical Process: Critical Factors for Strategic Success', Strategic Change, 10(4), 201–13.

Davis, S. and Davidson, B., (2020). *Vision: Transforming Your Business Strategy Today to Succeed in Tomorrow's Economy*, Simon and Schuster, New York, 1991.

Davis, S. M., *Future Perfect*, Addison-Wesley, New York, 1987.

De Geus, A. P. 'Planning as Learning.' *Harvard Business Review* (March-April 1988).

Dixit, Avinash K. and Nalebuff, Barry J., *Thinking Strategically: The Competitive Edge in Business Politics and Everyday Life*, W. W. Norton & Co., 1991.

Drucker, P. *The Practice of Management*. New York: Harper & Brothers, 1954.

Dyer, J. H., P. Kale and H. Singh. (2001). 'How to make strategic alliances work'. *MIT Sloan Management Review* (Summer): 37-43.

Dyment, J. J. 1987.'Strategies and management controls for global corporations'. *Journal of Business Strategies* (Spring): 20-26.

Edelman, B. (2014). 'Mastering the intermediaries. Strategies for dealing with the likes of Google, Amazon, and Kayak'. *Harvard Business Review* (June): 86-92.

Edelman, B. (2015). 'How to launch your digital platform: A playbook for strategists'. *Harvard Business Review* (April): 90-97.

Eisenhardt, K. M. and S. L. Brown. 'Competing on the Edge: Strategy as Structured Chaos'. *Long Range Planning* 31, no. 5 (1998): 786-89.

Friedman, T. L. (2006). The World is Flat. A Brief History of the Twenty First Century. Farrar, Straus & Giroux.

Fréry, F. (2006). 'The fundamental dimensions of strategy'. *MIT*

Sloan Management Review (Fall): 71-75.

Gaddis, J.L. (2005). *Strategies of Containment: A Critical Appraisal of American National Security Policy during the Cold War*. Oxford University Press: UK.

Gaddis, John Lewis (2005). *Strategies of Containment*. Oxford University Press.

Gates, B. and Hemingway, C. (1999). *Business @ the Speed of Thought*. New York: Warner Books.

Gilmore, J. and Pine II, B. Joseph. (1999). *The Experience Economy*. Boston: Harvard Business School Press.

Gladwell, M. (2005). *Blink, The Power of Thinking without Thinking*. New York: Little Brown & Company.

Guillen, M. F. and E. Garcia-Canal. (2012). 'Execution as strategy: How emerging-market multinationals thrive amid turbulence'. *Harvard Business Review* (October): 103-107.

Hamel, G., & Prahalad, C. K. (1989, May/June). 'Strategic intent.' *Harvard Business Review*, 63-76.

Hamel, Gary & Prahalad, C. K., *Competing For the Future*, Harvard Business School Press, 1994.

Harari, Y. N. (2015). *Sapiens: A Brief History of Humankind*. New York: Harper Collins.

Hinterhuber, H.H. & Popp, W. (1992, January-February Issue) 'Are You a Strategist or Just a Manager?'. *Harvard Business Review*. Retrieved from https://hbr.org/1992/01/are-you-a-strategist-or-just-a-manager

Kaplan, R. S., and David P. N. (1996). *The Balanced Scorecard: Translating Strategy into Action*. Boston: Harvard Business School Press.

Kelly, T. (1982). 'Thucydides and Spartan Strategy in the Archidamian War,' *American Historical Review*: 87, p 25-54.

Kim, W. C. and Mauborgne, R. (2005). *Blue Ocean Strategy*. Boston, Harvard Business School Press.

Lindgren, M. & Bandhold, H. (2009). *Scenario Planning: The Link Between Future and Strategy* (2nd ed.). Basingstoke: Palgrave Macmillan.

MacCoun, Robert J. (1998), 'Biases in the interpretation and use of research results' (PDF), *Annual Review of Psychology*, 49: 259–87.

McGrath, R. G. (2011). 'Failing by design'. *Harvard Business Review*, 89(4), pp. 76-83. Retrieved from https://hbr.org/

Miles, R.E., & Snow, C.C. (1978), *Organizational Strategy, Structure and Process*, McGraw-Hill: New York.

Montgomery, C.A. (2012, July). 'How strategists lead'. Retrieved from McKinsey Quarterly.https://www.mckinsey.com/business-functions/strategy-and-corporate-finance/our-insights/how-strategists-lead

Murray; et al. (1994). *The Making of Strategy: Rulers, States, and War*. Cambridge University Press. pp. 1–23.

Neumeier, Marty. Zag. *The #1 Strategy of High-Performance Brands*. Berkeley: New Riders, 2007.

Nobel, C. (2012, July 16). 'Are You a Strategist?' *Harvard Business School Working Knowledge*. Retrieved from https://hbswk.hbs.edu/item/are-you-a-strategist

Peters, Tom. *Thriving on Chaos*. New York: Wings, 1995.

Peters, Tom and Austin, Nancy. *A Passion for Excellence*. New York: Wings Books, 1995.

Penades, A. (2016 November/December issue). 'Bred for Battle— Understanding Ancient Sparta's Military Machine'. Retrieved from https://www.nationalgeographic.com/archaeology-and-history/magazine/2016/11-12/sparta-military-greek-civilization/

Porter, Michael. *Competitive Advantage: Creating and Sustaining Superior Performance*. New York: Free Press, 1985.

Ries, Al and Laura. *The Origin of Brands*. New York: Harper, 2004.

Phills, James A. Jr. *Integrating Mission and Strategy for Nonprofit Organizations*. Oxford: Oxford University Press, 2005.

Porter, M.E., *Competitive Strategy: Techniques for Analyzing Industries and Competitors*, Free Press: New York, 1980.

Porter, Michael E. 'What is Strategy?' *Harvard Business Review* (November-December 1996): 61-78.

Porter, Michael E. *Competitive Advantage: Creating and Sustaining Superior Performance*. New York: The Free Press, 1985.

Radhakrishnan, S. (2018, April 7). 'Trouble in India's Real Estate Market'. *International Policy Digest*. Retrieved from https://intpolicydigest.org/2018/04/07/trouble-in-india-s-real-estate-market/

Rangan, V. Kasturi. 'Lofty Missions, Down-to-Earth Plans,' *Harvard Business Review* (March 2004).

Rumelt, R. (2011). *Good Strategy/Bad Strategy: The Difference and Why It Matters*. London: Profile Books.

Russo, J. Edward and Schoemaker, Paul J. H., *Decision Traps: The Ten Barriers to B Decision-Making and How to Overcome Them*, Fireside Press, 1989.

Schartz, P., *The Art of the Long View*, Doubleday, New York, 1991.

Schrange, M., *Shared Minds: The New Technologies of Collaboration*, Random House, New York, 1990.

Senge, P. (1990). *The Fifth Discipline: The Art and Practice of the Learning Organization*, Doubleday: New York.

Sun, T. (1983). *The Art of War*, Dell Publishing: New York.

Tichey, N. M. (1983). *Managing Strategic Change: Technical, Political and Cultural Dynamics*, John Wiley & Sons: New York.

Treacy, M. (1995). *The Discipline of Market Leaders*, Addison Wesley: Reading, MA.

Tversky, A. & Kahneman, D. (1974). 'Judgement under uncertainty: Heuristics and biases'. *Science*. 185 (4157): 1124–1131.

Tweed, S. C. (1990). *Strategic Focus: A Gameplan for Developing

Competitive Advantage, Fel Publishers: New York.

Weisbord, M. R. (1987). *Inventing the Future: Search Strategies for Whole Systems Improvement*, Productive Workplaces, Jossey-Bass.

Wootton, S. and Horne, T. (2000). *Strategic Thinking: A Step-by-step Approach to Strategy*. New York: Kogan Page Publishers.

Yip, G. S. (1992). *Total Global Strategy: Managing for Worldwide Competitive Advantage*, Prentice Hall: New Jersey.